"A MASTERPIECE!"
—Andrew M. Greeley

Donny's true workout was not a fell-run at all. It was a devastating gymnastic display a thousand feet above the ground. He bounced from rock to rock in a dizzying succession of handstands and cartwheels. He spun and leapt, twisted and somersaulted like a circus aerialist gone beserk.

Jillian caught her breath, and lowered the binoculars. And was blind. It was too dark! Was he mad . . . ? How could he dare to do something like this?

PRAISE FOR *ACHILLES' CHOICE*

"A well-told tale that combines imaginative extrapolation (in this case, upon bioengineering and sports medicine) with a mystery . . . Absorbing."

—Booklist

"A welcome breeze of fresh air . . . both an intriguing and frightening logical extension of how society uses up its best and brightest."

—Rockland Courier-Gazette

"Mr. Niven has knack for making science fascinating to the layman, and he is gifted with a dry sense of humor that is always entertaining."

—Atlanta Journal-Constitution

ACHILLES' CHOICE

LARRY NIVEN

AND

STEVEN BARNES

A TOM DOHERTY ASSOCIATES BOOK
NEW YORK

This is a work of fiction. All the characters and events portrayed in this book are fictitious, and any resemblance to real people or events is purely coincidental.

ACHILLES' CHOICE

A Tor Book
Published by Tom Doherty Associates, Inc.
175 Fifth Avenue
New York, N.Y. 10010

Tor® is a registered trademark of Tom Doherty Associates, Inc.

Art by Boris Vallejo

ISBN: 0-812-51083-6

First edition: March 1991
First mass market printing: April 1992

Printed in the United States of America

0 9 8 7 6 5 4 3 2 1

ACHILLES' CHOICE

Chapter

I

Jillian Shomer ran along the north edge of the quarry, toward a distant, silent ocean, into the dawning sun. Her breath vibrated in her mastoid process, made sharp rasping sounds in her Comnet ear link. In her own very informed opinion, she sounded ragged and undisciplined.

Hot fudge sundaes are a basic food group. The words were etched in acid, her self-appraisal as merciless as the grade.

She unclipped the plastic bottle at her side, and sipped shallowly. Thin, faintly sweet, with a briny edge. The drink was custom-formulated from analysis of her own sweat, a nutrient solution composed chiefly of water and long-chain glucose polymers, with a few electrolyte minerals judiciously added. Jillian thought the sweat tasted better.

The air would heat soon. Morning chills burned off quickly of late, unusual for Pennsylvania in late March. April and May would be hot.

She squeezed the bottle closed with her teeth, and pushed onward. Halfway through now. Sean Vorhaus would be meeting her for the last two miles of the run. With the first tickle of fatigue her mind, ordinarily the most orderly of instruments, began to wander. She focused, and continued to dictate.

"Beverly: note. Mind seeks patterns. Predictions. Wrong here. Old math . . . says weather's chaotic. Initial conditions. Disease, money, whatever. Try crime. Greek poets, storm . . . metaphor for personal change. Proposal—"

She panted, and wiped away the trickle of sweat oozing from beneath her terry-cloth headband. Her breathing normalized swiftly, and she continued.

"—use fractals, predict—global sociopolitical patterns. Determine where chaos rules human life—"

Funny how concise these notes always were. When she was running, she couldn't spare the breath! An athlete training at a reasonable level should still be able to talk . . . and unable to sing; who was it tried *that*? And Beverly would edit out the gasping.

In print it would come out more like, "Although the human mind functions so as to seek patterns and predictability within chaos, the peculiar mathematics of my chosen field suggest that the only pattern ultimately discernible in weather is chaos itself. Weather is very sensitive to initial conditions, as is disease con-

trol, the relative value of currency, and whatever else I can come up with. This approach might be used to reduce crime rates. But note: the Greek poets used storms as metaphors for drastic changes in human existence. Proposal: although currently considered impractical, I believe that fractals can be used to predict global sociopolitical patterns. The trick is to determine the degree to which chaos itself is a controlling factor in human life—''

The path split and she automatically chose the high road. The old mine lay at the feet of the Allegheny mountains, and had once been a source of coal and natural gas.

Energy sources and environmental concerns had shifted drastically in the last hundred years. Thanks to the Council, there were probably forty billion tons of coal in the Pennsylvania earth that would never be harvested. How many tons of smog did that translate into? How many square miles of soot-stained lung tissue?

The deserted mine was an atavistic eyesore, a raw, mile-wide slash. Long ago, men had ripped coal from the earth, made it bleed black, carted away its flesh to heat homes and industrial furnaces. Today the Council had decreed cleaner sources: solar satellites, geothermal stations, fusion reactors.

The strip mine lay before Jillian, around her, a barren womb. Its grueling inclines and sudden, twisty depths were a challenge to mind and body, an ideal preparation for the rigors to come.

So lost in reverie was Jillian that she failed to hear Sean's familiar rhythmic stride until he was ten feet away.

Sean Vorhaus was taller than she, and broader through the chest, with a longer stride. But he was a sprinter, with a sprinter's power in his upper body. Jillian was built to run miles, not meters. Her other physical discipline added the torso muscle that made them an obvious social item around Pennsylvania Tech.

Sean's ruddy face glistened with sweat as he came abreast of her. They managed a quick, bumping kiss without breaking stride.

Ah, the glories of coordination.

"How's the hip this morning?" he asked.

"No more 'click click.' "

"Any word from Beverly?" He pointed to her Comnet. The Council might try to reach her now, she supposed . . . but she didn't expect any contact before noon. Even so, it was comforting to know that whenever or wherever the call came, whatever the answer was, she would know.

Their footsteps seemed to merge. "You know how I feel, Jill."

She nodded. The grade steepened. They took a seventy-degree sprint up a ridge of ash and shattered stone, breathlessly matching strides. Behind them the morning sun had cast a slender silvery wedge on the western rim of the quarry.

Day was here. Almost certainly their last together. No matter what the Council's decision, things could never be the same between them. Sean could never again be coach and mentor. Probably not lover. Perhaps not even friend.

A chill swept her, and she focused on the steady rolling stroke of sole against rock.

The incline leveled out. Jillian's breathing normalized swiftly. The dark, stony earth turned beneath her shoe, but she didn't stumble. Her ankles were strong. By both nature and nurture, her entire body was as durable and flexible as copper wire. She compensated, caught her balance, and ran on.

Sean brushed a lick of brown hair back from his forehead. "In a couple of hours . . . you won't be mine anymore."

I never was.

The thought reached her lips, but went no further.

Sean saw the tension of restraint, misinterpreted its meaning, and hushed what he thought would be a cloying endearment. "Let's"—he huffed for air—"not kid each other. Not now. You'll make the team. And you're going for the gold. Even . . . if you come back to Penn Tech, you'll be different. Linked. Just want you to know"—he puffed, sucking wind as she picked the pace up—"wouldn't have missed this for the world. All of this—"

She tried to speak again.

"Bullshit," he said amiably. "Save breath. Need it. Race you to the bikes."

He broke into a run. As always, she dredged up strength from somewhere in her reserves to follow him, match him. And as always, especially now, on this last of their days together, she was careful not to pass him.

*　　*　　*

There were classes scheduled at Pennsylvania Technical University, but no one expected Jillian Shomer to attend them. Not today.

She would wait for the word. Yes, or no. Go or stay.

Arm in arm they returned to her dorm room. They took a hot, leisurely shower together, sluicing away the perspiration, soaping each other's bodies lavishly. Her long hard *biceps femoris* muscles tingled as the warm pulsing water dissolved knots of tension.

And as they showered, Jillian's multifunction personal data Simulacrum Beverly analyzed her run. As always, Bev's critique was merciless and precise. As always, it was given in a cunningly programmed Southern lilt.

''—compensating for the grade, your stride altered to twenty-three inches.''

Jillian waited for the carefully crafted sounds of disapproval.

''Tsk, tsk, Jill. Is this the best you can do? We both know that twenty-five''—Beverly pronounced the number *twenny-fahve*—''is optimum for your height and present weight.''

Sean chortled. ''Bev slays me.''

''Energy,'' Jillian called, spitting water.

''Energy metabolism appears adequate . . .'' A pregnant pause. ''But you made a little mistake, honey.''

''And what was that?''

''When you tinkled this morning, I got a urine sample—''

Jillian grimaced, and whispered to Sean: ''Remind me to disconnect the toilet monitor.''

"Hah!"

"—and it looks to me like you snuck in a little snack since yesterday."

"Me? Me? How could you say such a thing?"

"Sugar," Bev said reprovingly. "Based on alkaloid content and protein chromatography, the contraband was most likely a hot fudge sundae."

"Guilty as charged. Bravo, Beverly."

"Jillian, dear child, your nutritional profile is solid enough to survive an occasional dalliance, but don't expect me to applaud."

Jillian toweled off as she left the shower, and watched as a holographic scan of her body appeared in the air before her. Pools of color-coded glitter swirled in the image, displaying circulation and muscle tension.

She lay stomach-down on her bed, eyes on the shimmering image. Sean knelt beside her.

His fingers were magical, easing knots of tension from places so tight they hadn't had room to scream. She rolled over, and her towel fell away.

At the age of twenty-three, Jillian Shomer still seemed to have baby fat along her jaw, unless she bit down hard to reveal the muscle protecting her neck. Her face, framed by short blonde hair, was too strongly angular to be sheerly decorative, softened only by eyes which were oak-brown with flecks of emerald. She might have been considered plain, except when smiling or talking. In much the same way, her body was too solidly muscled, her subcutaneous fat pared too finely for any classically feminine image. But when she was in motion . . .

Ah, that was quite a different thing. In motion, Jillian was liquid light, a symphony of power and grace, and ordinary standards simply didn't apply.

"Ultrasound analysis reveals a weakness in the left Achilles tendon, which is caused by tension in the right hip flexor."

"Suggestion?"

"Twofold. First, postpone your plyometric speed drills while we run institute rehabilitative lateral gastrocnemius exercise."

"Fine. And the second?"

Beverly paused, almost shyly. "Well, I'd recommend some form of massage to help your hips relax, honey. Maybe that big burly hunk of a man has some suggestions."

Sean guffawed, rolled her and scooped her into his arms. "Cheating!" he said. "That's what she *always* prescribes."

"We think alike is all. Right, Bev?"

"Humph. A Southern lady doesn't watch such goings-on."

"In that case, switch off."

"Have fun, children."

Sean and Jillian laughed together, and then quieted. How could they make this seem casual? Everything they said or did had a ring of finality to it.

"I don't want to look at the clock," she whispered.

He smiled. "What do you want?"

"Just hold me. 'Gird up thy loins now like a man . . .' "

"Huh?"

"Job thirty-eight, verse three."

"Pretty randy for a Bible verse." He brushed her lips with his, then nuzzled the nape of her neck until her breathing grew deep and ragged. "And what did it say after that?"

Her voice was thick, and swallowing was an effort. "Something about 'laying the foundations of the Earth.'"

"Ambitious."

She pressed herself against him. "Just hold me until they call. I don't want to think. I'll go crazy if I think."

He was good that way. They were good for each other, that way. For Jillian, he was the only one who had ever been able to stop the madness, stop the daydreaming, the endless carousel of thought.

Then why couldn't I belong to him?

Because I don't belong to myself.

For Sean, the future meant a position on the board of Penn Tech, tenure, publication, precious Comnet access time.

For her, the stakes were the whole world.

So they held each other until the wall rang, beckoning her back to reality. And safely cocooned in Sean's wiry arms, she heard the news she needed, feared, the words she hoped for.

When the glorious rows of Olympians marched in Athens, Jillian Shomer could well be among them.

And sometime between now and then, she would have to make a terrible decision.

Life. Death. Victory.
''Achilles' choice,'' Sean whispered.
And for the last time, they made love.

*   *   *

The being that called himself Saturn sat in his
Void, a spider crouched in the midst of an infinite web,
with strands that reached into every aspect of communication and information retrieval on Earth. Jillian
Shomer's name slid past his awareness, barely noted.
She was one of thousands of finalists from all over the
world. Many of them would make it to Athens. Few
would live to great age.

He couldn't afford to care, and didn't. In a few
seconds he scanned the entirety of her academic and
athletic career, calculated the odds against her, and
filed her away with the file flagged.

She really hadn't much of a chance. He would
watch her esthetic event, though. Her concept was ap-
pealing, one that he might have tried himself, long ago,
in another life.

Chapter

2

Sean's fingers touched her shoulders, the taste of his kiss still warm on her mouth. His eyes had left her face, were focused on the line of gleaming tube cars behind her. A pleasantly synthesized voice sang out the current stream of departures and arrivals for Pittsburgh Central.

She circled his waist, crushing herself against the hard bands of muscle. She fought to absorb him, impress him upon her memory: ice-blue eyes, thin firm mouth, black hair, Apollonian torso. A scent tinged with musk and fresh citrus. His heart pounded its languid rhythm, and hers sped to match it.

"We'll see each other again," he said finally.

"It won't be the same." Damn it, she had promised herself she wouldn't snivel.

"It never is." He tilted her chin up. "And who is it that taught me that?"

She managed a smile, went up to tiptoe, pressing her mouth against his again, lips parted, sealing their goodbye with a ferocity that shocked her.

Then she stepped back and, without another word, entered the nearest car on the Denver platform. She found a seat and threaded her ticket through the chair arm. The door closed behind her. The line of windowless cars slid forward, like the first moment of a roller coaster ride, down and down and down.

Part of her had expected the royal treatment, brass bands and ticker tape and a chorus of hallelujahs to wish her bon voyage. She felt utterly alone.

No one understood the isolation of total discipline. For ten years there had been little social life, less free time. Only the endless, grinding cycle of training and research. Ultimately, it had pushed even Sean to the outside.

At least she had Beverly. Beverly's personality core resided in an optical wafer in her wallet. She knew she was indulging her paranoia, but it was a conscious indulgence. Once in Denver she could hook back into Beverly's main banks through Comnet . . . but she had heard horror stories, and never traveled without a core. Beverly had been her cybernetic nursemaid, childhood friend, study partner, confidante, and lab assistant. Ultimately, Beverly had been the only shoulder for Jillian to cry on when her mother died eleven years ago.

She would not risk Beverly.

As she flashed within the earth, as weightless as

a lost ghost, she felt that aloneness more starkly. She seemed to be passing over an invisible meridian. More than time and distance were being traversed here. And if she made the wrong decision . . .

She squeezed her eyelids shut, and tried not to think for the rest of her seventy-minute ride. The train fell through the bowels of the earth at nearly orbital speed. Its silence was broken only by the thunder of her heartbeat as it returned, stroke by slow stroke, to its resting pace of forty-six beats a minute.

* * *

The Denver station was a honeycomb of concrete and stainless steel, so like the Pittsburgh depot that it was disorienting. The price of standardization. Transportation had built the depot, and the Council liked uniformity.

She looked out across the crowd, searching for a familiar face. Only strangers were to be seen, but in an odd way, they were family. In whatever city, whatever country, at whatever craft they toiled, more than at any other period in history, the citizens of Earth were one united people. These folk had never known the specter of war. Famine and pestilence were distant memories for most of them. These were the children of a new time, the first generation with the power to make a perfect world.

Most specifically, a world in which friction between its component parts was being reduced to something approaching zero.

By the time the Council had formed, less than 30

Larry Niven & Steven Barnes

percent of American adults were registered to vote, and less than 45 percent of those used the privilege. The nations of Earth were dying institutions, impotent relics of a more primitive age. And who really cared?

A cardboard placard held by pale slender fingers caught her attention. It said: JILLIAN.

She squirmed her way through the crowd.

The man holding the placard was thin—marathon-thin, his posture like a question mark, his facial bones too prominent. An age ago his bright boyish good looks had reached through a TV set to capture a young Jillian's heart. There wasn't much left of that. He had huge hands, their skin stretched so tight that they seemed amphibian. She pretended not to notice.

Booster-induced acromegaly. Within months he would be an utter grotesque. If he lived that long.

A thick belt around his waist was the only prosthetic system she could see. A microprocessing system in the belt performed millions of operations per second, communicating with implants in the owner's liver, pancreas, spine, heart, and brain. The massively invasive technique could slow, but not halt, the inevitable deterioration.

His mouth was unexpectedly warm and friendly. His eyes, gray-green, invited her to share a world filled with mischievous secrets. "Jillian Shomer?"

"Abner Warren Collifax?" Both were unnecessary questions.

He offered an arm. She took it, found it disconcertingly skeletal. "Come on. Your luggage is coded through already. It should be down the chute and in the car by the time we get there."

"Privilege?"

"You're one of the elite, and don't you forget it. I can guarantee you no one else will."

She liked him, his eyes and his thin tousled hair and most of all the way he had made peace with his awful burden.

The Denver station's standardized sweep of featureless, curving walls began to change as they approached the escalators. A kinetic wall tapestry shimmered in the tunnels, depicting a vista of iron-gray mountains speckled in white. As they boarded the escalator, the seasons changed. The white mantle grew thicker and whiter. Tiny skiers flew down the slopes.

Abner was one step ahead of her, shifting his weight uncomfortably from one foot to another: a touch of hyperkinesis.

Shyly, Jillian said, "I watched you four years ago, in your second Olympiad."

"You're surprised to see me still around?" He brayed laughter.

She was instantly embarrassed. "Pleased. Only four Americans have ever combined judo and fellrunning. I'm looking forward to working with you."

"If you still feel that way in nine weeks, I haven't been doing my job."

They emerged into an underground valet garage. Rows of electric cars gleamed in the artificial light, each nosed up to a charging post. Luggage was already coasting out of wall chutes. Jillian squinted, wondering which car might belong to this gangling man who had fought so bravely, and borne his second, terminal defeat with such courage.

A silver needle-wedge coupe glided up to them. Her bags had been piled into the back. Abner punched a tip into his wristlink, touched it to the pimply attendant's badge. The badge glowed and quietly said: "Thank you very much, Mr. Collifax. Most generous."

The attendant held the door for them. As they drove up the ramp, Abner chuckled. "You've got to wonder, don't you?"

"Wonder what?" The sunlight made her squint as they emerged into the open. Denver was intimidating. All glowing chrome and dull glass, crowding out life, a mutant forest clawing up into a cloudless sky.

"The attendant," Abner said after a pause so long her mind had wandered. "He programs his badge to thank you if you tip high. Maybe it curses you if you tip low. I can tip him without touching his hand. They've kind of got the people out of the loop, don't they?"

"You've got a weird mind."

"One of a kind." He grinned.

Ahead of them lay the Rocky Mountains.

* * *

Nestled into the foot of those slate-gray peaks was the Rocky Mountain Sports Research Facility, visible from ten miles away as a symmetrical array of domes and cubes. Jillian experienced a wave of déjà vu as they passed an angle identical to that of the airport mural. Then Abner glided on, and the moment passed.

"How are the academic facilities?"

"You'll find everything that you need. I don't think you'll need that p-core."

"Just the same—"

"Old friends are the best."

The car delivered them to the gate in four more minutes. It slid open at the silent urging of their guidance unit.

"Have you made a decision about the operation?"

The question was just a touch too innocent. She had been waiting for it, and was only surprised that it had taken so long to arrive.

"First, I want to see how I stack up." She chose each word carefully. "Just me. No modifications. I've been working on some noninvasive techniques of my own, and I'm hoping."

"Hope," he laughed. "I remember hope."

"It's alive and well."

"And living in obscurity."

He pulled up to her dormitory, a three-tiered beige cube. Only a pink and blue trim of hyacinths around the base gave it any semblance of grace. "We'll have a general meeting in about forty minutes."

"I'll be there. And thanks."

"Thank you," he said. Something that might have been pride flitted across that ruined face. "Thanks for asking for me."

"You're the best I could find, Abner. You were one of the greats."

"I'm also a dinosaur looking for a tar pit. Some people don't want me here. Maybe they don't want to be reminded." He ran thin fingers through thinner hair. "Anyway. Welcome to the death camp."

She slid her rucksack out of the back seat, then leaned her head in. "Abner?"

"Yes?"

"You don't resent it, do you?"

"I knew what I was doing, Jillian. Just . . ."

"What?"

Abner seemed to fight with himself, deciding how much of himself to share. "Well, I had two silvers and a bronze. The guy who beat me in academics delivered a paper on the relationship between illiteracy and crime. He claimed we could cut the crime rate by thirty percent just by rearranging the educational priorities in grade school. He took gold, that's how impressed they were."

"That must have hurt."

"*That* didn't." Some vast and distant pain floated behind his eyes. "The Olympiad is about finding the best and harvesting their knowledge and their genes. What hurt is that he was wrong. He had to have been wrong, because they never used it."

She stared at him. "Who was he?"

He paused, and then smiled crookedly. "Russian. Name of Pushkin. Dead now. He only took the one gold."

Ice touched the nape of her neck. *And Abner, too. Dying for lack of gold.*

They were both silent, and Jillian knew that he was about to leave. Before he could speak, she said, "Abner. The truth, okay? Knowing what you know now, would you do it again? Would you Boost if you were me?"

He leaned back into his seat. The clownish grin

disappeared. "Would I have your skill? Your basic talent?"

"Better still. You could have yours."

"This old man blesses you."

"Stop stalling. Would you take the Boost?"

He grinned crookedly. "In a hot second." And the car cruised away.

*　　*　　*

Jillian lugged her belongings into the building, up the stairs. A tickle of perspiration had wormed its way down her back by the time she reached the second level. Her footsteps echoed emptily in the deserted hallway. She heard distant shouts and thumps of exertion.

She leaned her forehead against one of the windows, and looked out over an outdoor track.

A battery of scanning devices were posted at sixteenth marks on a half-mile oval. Lithe figures jogged, sprinted, leapt. Her heart trip-hammered.

The fifty-foot ribbed dome to the east would be the sports medicine facility. There, her mind and body would be taxed to the maximum.

And over there . . . a converted dormitory, given now to . . . ?

"That's the academic center," a male voice said behind her. She spun to face a young man of perhaps twenty-five years. His massively muscular body strained at a gold-trim warm-up jacket. A soft, round face, with bright green eyes framed by extremely black hair. He was pushing a small covered cart.

"What?"

"That's the academic center," he said almost apologetically. "I figured that you were looking at it, and maybe wondering." He wiped huge hands on his red, white, and blue nylon sweat pants, and offered one to Jillian. "Hi. Jeff Tompkins."

"Jillian Shomer. I saw you at the last Olympiad. You went bronze, didn't you?"

His answering smile was shy, a little nervous. "Yeah. This is my last chance." He bit back some other comment, and muscles along the base of his jaw leapt.

"Ah—what's in the cart?" Jillian asked. That twitch at his jaw was fascinating. Now that she noticed it, it seemed to pulse regularly, like a little lizard running around under his skin.

He smiled sheepishly again, and lifted the lid.

Jillian sucked in her breath. "You did this?"

He nodded.

The marvel was perhaps seventeen inches along the base. Jeff Tompkins had carved an ivory model of a palatial estate, complete with towers and gardens and arches and miniature fountains, pillars and statues and even a tiny horse-drawn carriage at a miniature main gate.

"What in the world?"

"Oh," he said vaguely. "It's the palace built by Le Vau and Mansart for Louis XIV. At Versailles, of course." He pointed, his thick fingers so much larger than the miniature work that Jillian could hardly believe her eyes. "See here? The Cour d'Honneur, with little statues of Richelieu, and Du Guesclin, and Louis of course . . ." His voice grew absent. "The Cour Royale, and behind that the Cour de Marbre . . . the palace Chapelle was started by Mansart in 1699, but Robert de Cotte finished it . . . I need to touch it up. I was worried about how it would travel.''

''My God. It's boggling. How long . . . ?''

He shrugged. ''Four years. I started right after last Athens. I figured, you know, better go for it.''

She touched it gingerly. ''Elephant ivory . . . ?''

''Of course not. Mammoth. Part of the '17 Siberian excavation.'' A faint smile curled his thin lips. ''Well, better go. Welcome to the club, Jillian. I sure wish you the best of luck.'' He turned and headed down the hall, pushing his cart with its precious cargo.

Jillian watched Jeff until he disappeared around the corner, and then took her rucksack down to room 303. She nudged the door open with her foot.

A short black woman sat at a computer table. She wore cutoffs that exposed corded calves and thighs and a powerful upper body. Her tightly curled hair was cropped very short. When Jillian entered the room, the woman rose and spun with that liquid grace which implies perfect coordination. The shorter woman appraised her for a moment, and then grinned hugely.

''You must be Jillian Shomer. Fractals and judo?''

''And fell-running.''

A dark hand was extended to her. It was strong, and hard with callus. ''I'm Holly Lakein. Molecular biology and the balance beam. Chess. Do you play?''

''Not really.''

''Oh.'' She grinned, and waved a hand at the

computer table. A visual field projected a chess set composed of simple geometric shapes. When Holly's finger brushed a bishop, it skittered across the board to the next square. "Just reexamining Anderssen–Dufresne, 1852. Berlin. What they call the 'Evergreen' game. I think I've found a new response to the Queen Sacrifice that won the game."

Jillian smiled politely. "That must be very exciting."

"Yeah . . . well . . ." Holly shrugged. "Hell with it." She motioned toward a frame bunk on the far side of the room. "That one okay?"

"Sure." Jillian tossed her rucksack down on the bed, and watched under her arm as Holly floated to a closet, pulled down sheets and blankets, and tossed them to Jillian with a flip of her wrists.

Holly's economical perfection of movement was captivating, even applied to so mundane a task. Every joint seemed to be an oiled ball bearing; every exquisitely toned muscle moved in perfect sequence.

"When did you have it done?"

Holly grinned again. "Forty days ago. The Boost is peaking now, and will plane for the next month. Then we'll crank it up again. Hoping to hit Everest just about Athens."

"Aren't you scared?"

"Of course," Holly said. "But then again, my research is on the reversal or stabilization of the process itself."

"You mean . . . without Linking? I didn't think that was possible."

"Ask Abner."

*   *   *

The room was arched loftily. The light seemed to come from everywhere and nowhere, filtering down from the ceiling like a spray of moondust. Through the wall-wide windows Jillian could see the Rocky Mountains, their reality less vivid than a train station mural.

An irritatingly thin voice brought her attention back to the front of the room. The voice belonged to a tanned, slender woman whose sad eyes and pouchy cheeks reminded Jillian of a shaved housecat. "For those of you who don't know, I'm Dr. Andrea Kelly, your liaison with the Rocky Mountain Sports Medicine Facility. I would like to welcome all of you to the North American corporate and national training camp for the Eleventh Olympiad."

There was a polite smattering of applause. Jillian looked out over competitors nearest her, recognizing few of them. Most were faces without names. A few were faces and events.

There, sitting in a cluster on the left side of the room, was the track squad. Powerful but lean, they seemed as nervously alert as antelope in dry season. She tried to guess their modifications: artificial knee joints? Synthetic hemoglobin?

Near them were the power lifters, recognizable from their gigantic deltoids and the enormous sweep of the lats. The other Olympians avoided them. These monsters were Boosted, and on them the Boost had worked its most extreme miracle. Muscle and bone had thickened to a simian density. Their hands knotted and unknotted compulsively, and a palpable air of leashed aggression hung in the air about them.

From pictures in various scientific magazines she recognized faces: a discus thrower who specialized in underwater telecommunications. The article said his spine had been prosthetically restructured to allow greater torque. A regional lightweight women's power lifting champion with microprocessors implanted in the motor end plates of muscles in thighs and back. Her doctoral thesis had been immediately classified by World Security.

All looked to be between eighteen and thirty-two.

Andrea Kelly was still speaking. Her high, reedy voice barely needed amplification. "Everyone here understands the stakes. You have made serious decisions, sacrifices, lost jobs and friends, separated yourselves from family for the sake of our quest."

She paused.

Two seats down from Jillian, a blond, wiry light-weight wrestler muttered "*Our* quest? What you mean *we*, white man?" A black man next to the wrestler high-fived him, and there was a wave of nasty laughter.

"Three or four of you still have unresolved issues. This might be a good opportunity to discuss them."

A massive arm was raised on the other side of the room, and Dr. Kelly gave its owner the floor. Jeff Tompkins stood. He was wearing a cut-off shirt, and his musculature was even more pronounced. His upper arms and shoulders were a grotesque relief-map of veins and muscular striation. "I'm Jeff Tompkins."

"Hi, Jeff."

"Aum . . . Doc Kelly. A lot of us have already made our decision about Boost. I just want it out on the floor for the ones who haven't. Sometimes people Boost even when they don't have to. I throw the hammer, so I need the speed and power. But if you're not in a pure power sport, what are the chances of a gold or silver without the Boosting?"

"And just why do you care, Jeff?"

He looked at her with undisguised contempt. "You get your data whether we live or not. We're not l-lab rats you can use up and throw away. Like I said— I made my choice. I don't regret it. But for some of the others, it's the wrong damned choice."

Dr. Kelly tried to smile, and finally arranged her features in an expression of dignified neutrality. "The choice is more problematic for those of you who do not compete in a linear skill. In other words: how fast do you run, how high do you jump, how much can you lift? Those of you in gymnastics, wrestling, or fencing cannot just look at the record tapes and compare your performances with those of past gold and silver medalists. There's a gray zone.

"Most of your lives you've been surrounded by less gifted intellects, less developed bodies. If you have been involved in sports where strategy and skill are more important than simple speed or strength, you may question the value of Boosting.

"Let me answer your implicit question as explicitly as I can. If un-Boosted, regardless of whatever other modifications you may have made to your muscles, nervous system, or skeletal structure, you will be competing with Olympians who have a fifteen to twenty percent advantage over you in both the physical and psychological realms.''

The young man fidgeted, shifting from side to side in a manner reminiscent of a small child. Finally, he said, ''Yeah. That's what I wanted to hear.'' And he sat down.

There was a ripple of sound. One of the wrestlers stage-whispered ''Buck-buck-buckawwk!'' and somebody halfheartedly shushed him.

Jillian stood.

''Doctor,'' she said. ''As long as the floor is open, I have a question, too. The point of the Olympiad is to select the best. Why confine the definition of 'best' to those willing to risk death or disablement within nine years? That has always troubled me.''

Andrea Kelly's eyes bored into her. ''Well, ah . . . Jillian . . . You're the newest one here, and of course this discussion has come up several times before. The Olympiad is for those with enough confidence in their own abilities to risk everything. That peculiar, uncoachable capacity for confidence produces champions. Enables a human being to put everything on the line. That's one definition of a 'warrior,' isn't it? Well, we don't have wars anymore. But some people still need, and want, to test themselves against the very best.'' She smiled brilliantly. ''Confusion aside, I know you're one of those people, or you wouldn't be here, Jillian. To those who will risk much, much will be given.''

Dr. Kelly seemed to expect applause, and waited

for it. After a pause there was a polite smattering, but she was clearly uncomfortable.

Jillian waited until even that small accolade had died. "I see," she said, and sat down.

Dr. Kelly nervously scratched an ear, looking out at a group which was unexpectedly still. The room seemed to grow warmer. She cleared her throat. "Tomorrow," she offered, "our special guest will be Donny Crawford."

There was a murmur of recognition and approval from the audience. Jillian's reaction was instantaneous, and visceral.

The honey-gold perfection of his body in motion, dismounting from the uneven parallel bars. The deceptively boyish manner which masked a startling clarity of thought. The dark blue of his eyes as he accepted the gold in memory of those who had died in its pursuit.

She remembered him as he stood four years ago, straight and tall before a Council-appointed panel, carefully explaining the mathematical model for worldwide air traffic control. He had revolutionized consumer aeronautics with that one talk. He had competed in four events, won three gold and one silver. She guessed that maybe fifty million female viewers would have had a baby with him then and there.

Why be sexist? Probably ten million men had considered it, too.

Donald Crawford had made it. He was one of the few whose gamble had paid off. Those fifteen to twenty per Olympiad were paraded before the public once or twice a year, with great ceremony.

Those who failed to make it at their first Olympiad smiled bravely and trained like fiends. Those who failed a second time . . .

Like Abner?

. . . presently died.

3

"**Test run**," Jillian said crisply. She slipped Beverly's core into her desk console, and waited. And waited. Presently a distant voice said: "Jillian?"

"Right here, Beverly."

"You just wait there a minute, sugar. I was in the shower."

Making adjustments to the system, she meant. "I've got all the time you need," Jillian said.

Holly was concentrating on her chessboard, but when Jillian broke away from the installation procedure, her roommate picked up the broken threads of their conversation. "So . . . where were we? Neurotransmitters?"

"Right."

Holly ticked off names on her fingers. "Choline, acetylcholine, dopamine, all that crowd. The communications brigade. The thing you've gotta understand is that your survival is based on staying balanced between extreme states. It's a weird equilibrium—"

"Just a minute. I'm starting to get something here."

The visual field flickered, and Jillian was looking at her own face. The mirror-Jillian's skin dissolved, leaving a glowing skull. Bone followed, until a disembodied brain bobbled in the middle of the field. A chair appeared beneath it, tilted onto two legs. The brain balanced on top of the chair. Incandescently brown eyes popped from the ends of the optic nerves.

"Beverly, that's disgusting."

"But roughly accurate," Holly chuckled. "She's trying. You must have a fun Void."

"I'll wring her neck. Anyway, you were saying?"

"Boost tinkers with the balance, makes your brain select performance over health."

The field changed. The brain grew stork legs, began jumping through circus hoops. The hoops caught fire, and calliope music began to play in the background.

"I think Beverly is fully installed," Jillian said wryly.

"Have her access the files on Boost."

"All right. Test, Beverly. I need effects of Boost on the human nervous system."

The field pulsed with blue fog. "Long and short term?" her Simulacrum's voice asked.

"Yep."

"Multiphasic. Most noticeably a massive release of androgenic growth hormones. This effect takes months." As Beverly spoke, more crispness and personality filled her voice.

"Expect an increase in aggression and in coordination. There are mental effects. Clarity and speed of thought increased up to fifty-two percent. An average of twenty-five percent."

"Thanks, Bev. That's all for now."

Jillian shut the unit down.

She scanned the room, and thought it small but comfortable. All of her clothing was stored away, chairs and tables rearranged, and it was starting to feel like home. With Beverly now installed, Jillian felt she was ready . . .

"What are you thinking?" Holly asked.

"I don't know. Boost, maybe. It sounds so good."

"And costs so much. For about eight years you're a superman. It's probably twice as good as any other ergonometric technique. Or any *combination* of techniques, for that matter. Then, surprise! Your own body eats you."

"But you Boosted anyway, Holly."

"Yeah, but I'm looking for loopholes. It's a mug's game for the rest of you. Cancer, epilepsy, acromegaly. You get just two chances to go for gold, Jillian. Achilles didn't get much of a choice."

Holly returned to her chess game. Jillian sank down into her chair, and listened to her thoughts for a minute. She had not yet Boosted. She'd have to choose soon.

The tale was told to three billion TV sets during

every Olympiad. The gods had offered Achilles a short, glorious life, or a long dull one. He chose glory . . .

Behind her, Holly screamed ''Mate!''

*   *   *

While she immersed herself in her morning workout, Jillian watched the others in the gym. Their bodies had that telltale Boosted angularity. Jillian walked out onto the mat, her new judo *gi* crisp and just a little scratchy against her skin. Her black belt was knotted carefully, the white threads pale beneath the frayed surface. A worn black belt implied that the practitioner was more experienced.

She remembered when she first earned her *dan* ranking, and the evenings she had rubbed her new, starchy belt against cement, dipped it in bleach, sliced it shallowly with razors, trying to prematurely age her symbol of rank. She found the memory embarrassing, not funny. *Poor strategy. Strive to be underestimated!* What had old Sun Tsu said? ''At the beginning, be as coy and frightened as a maiden. Then when the enemy gives you an opening, rush in and crush him.''

Abner approached her with the same oddly disconnected movement he had displayed at the train station, like a puppet suspended from rubber bands instead of strings. Sometimes it was hard to believe he had been one of the top judo players in the world.

''Are we ready to work today?''

''Let's get to it.''

He gave her a swift visual inspection, and nodded curtly. Abner led her out onto a mat sandwiched with pressure sensors. The air shimmered with an I/O field, recording all actions as well as projecting whatever illusions might be necessary to evoke maximum performance.

Her opponent might have been a human being, so carefully was its appearance crafted. One could barely see the third leg, a slender stalk that projected to the rear to maintain balance. Its face was robotically neutral.

Jillian touched it, felt the balance. She inspected the fingers and hands, noting the hydraulics, the servomotors, the magnetic locks that would cling to the layer of foil in her *gi*.

With the slightest of hissing sounds, it bowed to her.

She giggled.

"Worked on a Grappler Twelve before?" Abner asked.

"No, but we had a Nine available to us at P. Tech."

"The Grappler Twelve has faster reflexes, and a better grip—you're webbed up under your *gi*? Otherwise it won't really be able to grasp you."

"Yes. We can do a check."

"We're going to be evaluating you for strength, balance, and coordination. Speed and endurance will be checked later, against a live opponent."

"Ready," Jillian said.

Balanced on its skeletal third leg, the Grappler moved in. Jillian extended her hands, and they gripped each other's sleeves, the Grappler's magnetic fingertips locking to the foil layer of her *gi*. The webbing that cocooned her body and attached it to the inside of the *gi* worked perfectly: the Twelve's grip was much more convincing than a Nine.

Jillian pivoted, slid her hip inside, and performed a perfect *ogoshi* hip throw. The Grappler flew over her back and crashed into the mat. Its legs contracted and extended, gyros whirred. It righted itself in less than two seconds, and was back.

This time Jillian used a *deashiharai* foot sweep. The Grappler did a clever little dance, and came very close to reversing the move.

She lowered her hips, dropping her center of mass. The Grappler suddenly went top-heavy, easy to upend and smash into the mat.

She was enjoying herself.

Abner watched, no hint of clownishness on his face, no laughter in his eyes as he watched the vectors play out in holographic display.

The test went on and on. Throwing, being thrown, coming to grips and taking the Grappler to the mat. There the robot was weak on technique, but compensated with awesome leverage.

Pushing herself now, she tied it up in a succession of mat holds and chokes, and forced it to beep submission three times.

At the end of an hour, Jillian was sopping wet, and blowing for air.

"Very good," Abner said blandly. "Now I think it's time for a human opponent."

"What?"

He smiled evilly. "The Grappler is decent for a readout or a warm-up, but there's nothing like a little honest human flesh."

Jillian was still gasping as he led her to another mat. A very blond woman two inches shorter than Jillian waited there. "I want you to meet Osa Grevstad. She's going to work with you today."

Although shorter, Osa was heavier through the shoulders. They probably weighed the same.

Her hair, cut short, did little to offset the butchiness of her overall appearance: hard, springy muscle, heavy bone structure, a level of energy so high she seemed to vibrate. Her eyes were slightly bloodshot, a frequent symptom of Boost.

Osa's face tightened as she smiled. There was humor but no warmth there. "You are the American who does not need Boost. We will see."

Jillian glared at Abner, not appreciating this at all.

The two women bowed and circled each other, moving into position. Their fingers sought grips on the *gi* sleeves as their hips twitched in feint, and they cat-stepped for position. Osa's hands changed positions as lightly as butterflies.

Abner's right, she had to admit. *There's nothing like human flesh.*

Osa spun tightly and went into *ogoshi* hip-throw position. Halfway into position she dropped lower, extended her leg to scythe Jillian's knees.

Jillian somersaulted into the throw, curled into a ball except for the hand that gripped Osa's shoulder and the foot that tucked into the blonde's gut. As Jillian hit the mat her own momentum heaved Osa up in a devastating *tomoenage* stomach throw. Osa flipped like a gymnast, but landed on the balls of her feet in perfect balance. She grinned, and said "Meow."

Jillian had never seen anyone move that fast, but controlled her awe: she also noticed that Osa's reflexes were slightly faster than her coordination. *Sometimes Boost changes things too quickly.* And *that* fact Jillian could use to her advantage.

The two women circled each other. Osa smiled. "You're very good, for one so timid."

"I detect an accent."

Jillian feinted a hip throw. Osa stiff-armed her back. "Yes. Born in Sweden, but I am Agricorp, not national!" she said proudly. "There were too many Judoka in Scandinavia."

"Somebody pulled some strings?"

Osa danced to the left, then right, almost catching Jillian in a foot sweep as she adjusted position. "Transferred my union files to a fishery in Seattle. It was easy to make the North American team. Your judo is not so good as ours."

Jillian started to protest, and suddenly Osa was gone, had disappeared under her, and Jillian was swinging in an explosively tight arc into the mat. She slapped hard, still had the breath jarred out of her. Then Osa was on her, grinding Jillian's face and chest into the mat, cranking her arms back, going for the pin.

The woman was everywhere at once, swarming, shifting, tireless.

It took everything that Jillian knew to keep Osa off, and she would have, if there had been a time limit.

But it went on, and on, a blurred, sweaty nightmare of fevered effort and ragged, shallow breaths. Osa seemed to grow stronger as the minutes passed, while

Jillian, already fatigued by the bout with the Grappler, came closer and closer to complete exhaustion.

The room swam. Her throat spasmed for breath, and her stomach knotted as she rolled over onto her side. The room began to swim, and Jillian's head pounded with pain. She felt totally disoriented.

Where was Osa? Had she given up?

Osa was grinning at her. Abner's arms were around her, and he peered into her eyes, concerned.

My God . . . she thought bleakly. *I've been choked out.*

Abner shook his head. "You better stop being so proud, tap out faster. Osa's pretty deadly with her *hadaka-jime,* isn't she?"

Jillian shook her head ruefully, and tried to roll over. Osa was standing, her arm around another girl, and they were smirking at her.

"Are you—"

"I'm fine," Jillian said.

"Jillian!" Osa called. "The Council might take a few Nationals to Greece. We need towel girls."

Jillian started to go for her. With sudden, unexpected strength, Abner pulled her back, herded her to the door of the shower room. "It's all right, Jillian. I learned what I needed to know."

"What? If I snore?"

He laughed. "I needed to know if you'd quit. You were beaten from the start, you know. I set you up. And you never quit."

The fatigue and frustration were almost too much. She started to say something, and felt her voice catch in her throat, looked quickly downward. To her surprise, he encircled her shoulders, and hugged her quickly. To her even greater surprise, she liked it.

"I've definitely got time for you, Jillian. Go on. Get dressed."

She smiled uncertainly, and then fled toward the distant smell of steam and soap.

4

Even her aching bones couldn't distract Jillian from the excellence of the Rocky Mountain Center's training table. Dinner was plentiful fresh fruit and vegetables, pasta and rice and chicken.

But despite the unity of purpose (everybody needed calories), there wasn't a real air of camaraderie. Even here, the awful risks of their shared venture dampened high spirits.

Holly sat next to her, picking at her meal with mantislike grace. Despite the delicacy of her movements, food vanished from her plate with astonishing rapidity.

"Still sore?"

"Globally." Jillian glared at a roasted thigh, mentally labeled it *Osa* and sank her teeth into it. "I think I've got a few ideas for the Ice Queen, next time around."

"She was first alternate on the Scandinavian Trials last Olympiad, when she was only sixteen."

"Slightly advanced, isn't she?"

"One word for it. Bet she suckered you into talking to her."

Jillian glowered, and Holly laughed heartily. "Yeah, I knew it. I heard some rumors about how she switched from Scandinavia to North America Agricorp so easily."

Jillian searched the room until she found Osa, sitting in the midst of a group of husky young men and women, laughing, attacking her food ravenously.

"Rumors? I thought the Council recognized no national boundaries, and all that."

"Baksheesh never hurts."

Osa looked up, locked gazes with Jillian, and smiled expansively.

Jillian broke eye contact.

Holly laughed. "She's beaten you already, you know. Got you hexed, but good."

A protest died on Jillian's lips as a fanfare blared over the cafeteria's speaker system. Dr. Kelly's voice broke through the static. Normally acerbic, it fairly bubbled with excitement. "Your attention please. Donny Crawford's shuttle has just requested permission to land. He will arrive in approximately one minute."

Every head in the room swiveled toward the windows.

Crawford swept down in an electric-blue float car, the air beneath the car distorted by a haze of heat and turbulence. A ramp unfolded, touched the ground, and three men stepped out.

Donny Crawford, and the usual Council bodyguards.

A sigh ran through the room as he trotted to the mess hall, flanked by the bodyguards, who were themselves minilinked to his security system. Their constant visual inspection of the grounds would be augmented by the electronic and satellite scans of the entire area. They were 360-degree-alert. It was difficult to imagine anything getting through that screen.

The security was understandable. Donny was high-level Linked, a candidate for the Council now. If his area of expertise had been political science or economics rather than the pure sciences, he might already control serious power.

The external door opened, and he was there, haloed by fading sunlight, radiant.

Striding to the front of the room, he was beautiful, by carriage and visage more effortlessly charismatic than she could have dreamed. The room's strained, competitive air dissolved.

She had never been so close to a Linked before. Jillian felt a sudden yearning that shocked and dismayed her with its intensity.

He smiled brilliantly. "I just showed up a little early. Thought I'd join you for dinner. Looks good from here."

"Looks better than it tastes!" somebody yelled.

"We'll see. Listen, everybody—after you've finished eating, I'd like to get to know as many of you as possible. We're having an informal get-together, all workouts and coaching sessions canceled for the evening."

Thank God.

With a healthy wave of applause, the trainees launched back into their dinners.

Jillian chewed thoughtfully. She watched Donny as he went to the head of the food line, piling his tray high.

"So what do you know about this guy?" Holly said conspiratorially.

"Well, I know he's gorgeous."

Holly's nod of agreement was emphatic. "I wonder if he can be made. I don't know how much time he's got. Or I've got . . ."

"Whoa, girl. Back, back. Rein in those hormones."

"You don't believe any of that bull about sex being bad for your athletic performance?"

"Well," Jillian mused, "I'm not saying having sex during training is a felony . . ."

"That's nice to hear."

"It's more like a misdemeanor: the more I miss, demeanor I get."

Holly laughed until Jillian had to slap her on the back. It felt like slapping a truck tire.

After dinner was over, they retired to the meeting hall next door. Tables and chairs were arranged in starbursts.

Crawford circulated through the room shaking

hands, smiling, flirting, talking shop. Jillian saw nothing overtly peculiar about his hairline . . .

Beneath Donny's hair a wire mesh had been implanted in the scalp. Metal strands only a few molecules thick extended into various areas of his brain. They controlled the firing of neurons and synapses, and regulated many of the biological functions that Boost had disrupted. That was Donny Crawford's way out: as long as he remained Linked, the side effects of Boost wouldn't damage him.

Finally, his circuitous palm-pressing route brought him to Jillian.

His smile was beneficent. "Jillian Shomer. I've wanted to meet you."

"Yes," she said clumsily, instantly embarrassed. The only other reply that flashed into her mind was, *We'd make beautiful babies.*

"Well, I think you're going to show us something special."

It was an act of physical control to keep her reply out of the realm of the suggestive. "I'm in fell-running. Intervals, broken-ground, obstacles, and so on."

His eyes crackled with secret amusement. "Yes, I know."

Wasn't there any place they could be alone? "I hear that you mix some free-climbing into your workouts."

"I'm looking forward to the Rockies," he said, breathing deeply. "The air is thin, and very clean— should be a good burn."

She lunged into what she hoped was an opening. "Is there any chance that we could get together?"

"No, I'm afraid not. There's really no time."

She nodded. Gods cannot sport with mere mortals.

The Greek gods did!

And mortals suffered for it.

Donny moved on. As if an envelope of intimacy had ruptured, suddenly she heard other conversations around her, saw other faces. Her cheeks flushed red.

To heck with the rules. Come what may, she *had* to see more of him.

* * *

The sun hadn't risen yet.

Jillian had been awake since three-thirty. She lay on a tarp, watching the guest dorms through a pair of infrared binoculars borrowed from Holly.

She knew from vidzine articles that Donny Crawford got in his first workout of the day before dawn.

The binoculars put a misty red haze over everything, but through that haze, outlines were amazingly sharp. She wore a thermal warm-up suit to protect her from the cold. Still, she stretched and wiggled continuously to keep the juices flowing.

A creaking sound, a brief glimmer of light against the back of the building, and he emerged.

Donny stretched each leg briefly, twice, as though he had one of those infuriating bodies that never needed warming up. She kept the binoculars on him, let him get almost out of sight, and then began to follow.

So smoothly did he run that his feet barely seemed

to skim the ground. He was the best of the best. Even though this was a light maintenance run at an unaccustomed altitude, it was all Jillian could do to keep him in sight.

He headed up into the mountain, up a narrow trail until the path slanted so steeply that it was almost impossible for her to stay hidden.

He had all but disappeared into the vertical face of the mountain when the true miracle began. As he warmed up, he began to hop from one rock to another, with an uncanny, spring-steel leap reminiscent of a giant flea.

Back and forth, with absolute balance, limitless endurance, and explosiveness that would have broken long-jump records with contemptuous ease, Donny Crawford worked into the true heart of his morning routine.

She'd never seen movement like that before, wasn't sure that *anyone* outside the Linked had ever seen it.

His true workout was not a fell-run at all. It was a devastating gymnastic display a thousand feet above the ground. He bounced from rock to rock in a dizzying succession of handstands and cartwheels. He spun and leapt, twisted and somersaulted like a circus aerialist gone berserk.

She caught her breath, and lowered the binoculars. And was blind. It was too dark! Was he mad . . . ? How could he dare to do something like this?

This, then, this range of physical capacities that bordered on the superhuman, was an aspect of Linking that no one knew. Her head spun.

She put the binoculars back to her eyes, marveling again.

Why didn't they *tell* people about this?

It all changed in an instant.

Donny's hands seemed to give way. He slipped, scrambled to catch himself, twisted madly for balance. He hit the rock heavily and collapsed.

For a moment she thought that it was just another move, the horseplay of an insanely overconfident acrobatic clown. Then she focused in on him. Donny was curled into a fetal ball, gripping his head with both hands, inches from a sixty-foot drop. In the still of the morning she could hear him moan.

Or was it only the wind? But he was thrashing like an infant, in directionless panic. Something had gone terribly wrong. He couldn't get down off the rock.

She moved up toward him, choosing her steps carefully. She couldn't move as quickly as he had, but she still scrambled with panic speed, as if her own life were in danger, or as if she were running for gold.

He rocked back and forth, crooning to himself, his mindless, agonized writhing bringing him too close to the rim of the ledge.

When she reached him he was trembling, his body almost off as she pulled him back by his ankle and held him. He was cold and wet, his entire body quivering as with a terrible fever.

"McFairlaine's goddamned two points," he wailed. His eyes were wide and feverish; his voice was a wavering high-pitched song. "Bastards. Bastards. Kill me for McFairlaine's two points . . ."

She slipped her arm around him, and he clung to her like a drowning man.

The sun was just cresting the horizon, but there was enough light for them to pick their way back down. Her shoulder and back burned with the strain. Twice she almost turned her ankle, and once they slid half a dozen feet before she caught her balance.

The tendons in his neck bulged and twitched. His face was a patchwork of strained muscle, a flowing horrific mask. He stared at her, still not knowing who she was or where they were. He sounded like an angry child. "Couldn't *be* a war if *he* did something, old bastard. McFairlaine wouldn't have pushed Energy if *he'd* come down from fucking Olympus and . . . just . . ."

His voice faded as he finally seemed to grasp his situation. His eyes cleared, his face straightened: Donny was back.

He gripped her shoulders, and swung her around. There were no thanks in his look, only panic. Too much panic to remember niceties. "What did I say?"

She rested, panting. "I wasn't really listening. I was too busy—"

"*Listen to me now.* Don't tell anyone what happened. And forget anything that you heard."

"Aren't you sick?"

"No. Don't tell anyone." His grip tightened. His fingers clamped her arm like steel prods.

"Are you worried what people might think?"

"It's not for me," he said. "It's for you. If they think you know . . ." Something terribly urgent gleamed in his eyes. "Just don't. You shouldn't have been there. This has nothing to do with you."

"You mean, you were expecting it?"

"Just . . . forget what you saw. What you heard." He breathed deeply. "I'll go back to the dorm alone. Don't let anyone see you, all right?"

He seemed to have recovered. He set off down the trail, even making a jaunty imitation of his former confident stride.

"Hey," she called after him. "You're welcome."

There was no reply.

*   *   *

Shomer again. Saturn's lips curled in a smile. Courage and foolhardiness have much in common. In fact, the difference may be nothing but perspective. Donny Crawford had great intelligence, great athletic gifts, and no courage at all. He'd only Boosted after cold-blooded calculation revealed an eighty-seven percent chance of winning triple gold.

Her emotional attachment to Crawford implied vulnerability, lack of control, and unpredictability . . . any of which, in the right situation, could be of use.

Besides, she amused him.

The old bastard?

If she only knew.

For .24 seconds he considered her, and Crawford, and the idiot McFairlaine and the implications of Energy's actions. They had been predictable, and within context even reasonable, but McFairlaine needed perspective.

Could McFairlaine be Feral? Sometimes one of the Linked, drunken with power, might step across an in-

visible line. To be Linked meant not only power in the external world, but growing control over your every mental process and sensation. Easy to sink into catatonic indolence or solipsistic power fantasies. To go Feral.

Saturn had to consider possibilities: an embolism for McFairlaine, or perhaps a lethal power surge. The extreme irony of that approach appealed to Saturn.

Not yet. Monitor McFairlaine. Give him his chance . . . for a while.

Chapter

5

"In Matthew 26:11 Jesus said that the poor will always be among us," Jillian said. Her words appeared as white strokes upon a blue visual field. They floated in the air like crisply perfect skywriting.

"And in that sense, he may have been the first theorist in the social applications of fractal geometry.

. *"The concepts of cognitive dissonance and the inevitable breakdown of communication therefrom have been understood for centuries. However, the unavoidable disintegration of systems as those systems become more complex and unwieldy has rarely been considered within a sociological lattice."*

She stopped for a moment, thinking and sipping cocoa. Sunlight filtered through the dorm window at an oblique angle. Despite the intensity of her concentration, the external world intruded. The air reverberated with the grunts and heavy footfalls of Olympians training outside.

Jillian had taken the day off from her grueling athletic schedule, protesting a sore hip.

It wasn't her hip that was sore, it was her head. The headache had been a continuous thing, sometimes hovering in the background, sometimes thundering into her mind like a crazed animal, destroying calm and thought and sleep. And every pulse was Donny Crawford. Donny falling, Donny sick and weak on the ledge. Beautiful, perfect, confident Donny whimpering into the morning darkness.

Jillian was afraid. But worse than that, she was confused.

"Even surrounded by the greatest wealth and comfort, a human being will experience a measure of irritation. Confined in the most squalid and demeaning circumstances, he will find some small thing to take pleasure in.

"This trait, and others, make it impossible to eradicate the final bit of chaos from our minds, as well as our social systems. The powers which govern . . . one might even say oppress . . ."

Oppress?

Did the Council *want* a certain amount of suffering? More than the absolute irreducible minimum?

"Couldn't be a war if he did something, old bastard."

Leave it for the moment.

"A stable society functions much like an organism, with communications between the organ systems, the organs, the tissue structures, the cells, and the organelles. As instruc-

tions flow from one level to another, and the inevitable distortions in communication accumulate, what happens?

"At the top, a plan may be shaped to provide the greatest good for the greatest number. But no plan conceived at one end of the spectrum can take into account all of the individuals at the other end. It simply is not possible—there is too much breakdown in communication along the way. Conversely, any system which is modular enough to deal intimately with those at the bottom is too unwieldy to be governed from the top."

She stopped, rubbing her temples fiercely.

"Fortunately for those who govern, the appearance of fair play is more important than the reality. At least that's what Machiavelli thought."

She looked at the words she had dictated, and knew what the headache had been about, and knew what she was about to ask Beverly to do.

God help her.

Carefully, with somber formality, she drew a mesh headset of wires, microphones, and black oval pads from a sandalwood box on her desk.

She prepared the apparatus: plastic electrode pads which clung snugly to her temples. Earphones. A combination throat mike and sensor. Dark eyecups like lightweight goggles.

"Void, Beverly."

* * *

Anyone Linking into the Void must create her own kinesthetic analogy. For one it might be the Library of Congress, crammed to the skylight with talking books.

For another, being seated in a vast lecture hall surrounded by experts who had the precise answers to all questions. Jillian's programming teacher had taken her own image from literature: Gormenghast, an immense, sprawling castle-city of a million infinitely varied rooms.

The adult mind was too rigid, its worldview too set, to build such an analogy. It must be created in childhood; but after that, it grew.

Jillian closed her eyes and breathed deeply ten times, with each breath sinking into a world of total relaxation, a specialized trance leading to the Void state.

The earphones hummed gently. Breathing. Heartbeat sounds, slowing. The purr of breakers against a shore. Synthesized into and among those sounds was a chorus of voices too distant to be consciously perceived. Lights flashed in her goggles, so dimly and quickly that she could never focus upon them. At her temples, tickles of pressure and electricity buzzed and caressed her skin, eased her into a state combining deep relaxation and total awareness.

Gradually the speckles of light congealed into searchlights playing through a fog. Then smoky swirls of color, and she was in her Void, in a mental ocean of layered oils, a phantasmagoria of sensation created by the union of an exquisitely conditioned mind and a dozen seamlessly orchestrated channels of sensory input.

The water cleared. Only a few varicolored fish, dazzlingly bright, betrayed the chaos beneath the tranquil structure of her illusion.

She sank through the depths until she felt sand and shells beneath her feet. A dolphin playfully nosed against her, and then scooted away into the murk.

She walked along the ocean floor toward a ring of shattered coral reefs. This was her place. In the reef was set an ancient and barnacle-encrusted door, the entrance Beverly had created for her fifteen years ago.

The door yielded to her touch. In the middle of the ring stood a chair, and a wooden grade-school desk. Carved names and slogans had been added over the years; otherwise the desk hadn't changed since Jillian's seventh birthday.

Seated in it, awaiting her, was Beverly.

Beverly wore a frilly white sundress, barely ruffled by the tide. Her high cheekbones were those of Lilith Shomer, Jillian's mother. Her heavy brows and strong mouth were mapped from Gregory Shomer, Jillian's father. Her hair was blond with a gleam of fine copper threads. Her eyes were a deep and tranquil brown.

Beverly smiled. "Jillian, darling. What do we need today?" Her voice was honeyed with a Carolina lilt.

Jillian's accessing of Beverly took the external form of a conversation, a conversation that existed out of ordinary time. Her talks with Beverly seemed to last for hours or days, but upon emerging from trance she invariably learned that only minutes had passed, minutes during which a vastness of information had entered her long-term memory.

Jillian sat down opposite. Emblazoned on the desk was a fifteen-year-old carving. It read: JILLIAN LOVES. Jillian kept changing the name following "loves." She'd finally left it open.

She was home. She relaxed to a degree inaccessible in her waking state.

Where to start? "I need to know about Donny Crawford."

Beverly smiled tolerantly. "The same Donny Crawford you've been mooning over for four years?"

"The same. We finally met. He went through some kind of fit this morning during his exercise up on the mountain. He said strange things, babbled about 'war.' He cautioned me not to tell anyone. My first guess is that his Link with the satellite broke."

Beverly's eyes dropped to her desk. A moment later she said, "Satellites EE23 and EE08 both went off line at five fifty-two local. Energy is blaming both events on random meteoric debris. EE23 will have to be replaced."

"Is Donny *that* dependent on satellite Links?" It was something she'd suspected; it was one argument against Boost. Donny had *won*. Even if Jillian won gold, she'd be a hybrid, a cyborg, magnificent but fragile . . .

Beverly's mouth opened to speak, then closed. Jillian felt something like a vast, compulsive yawn rack her body, and—

Jillian stood before an ancient and barnacle-encrusted reef. In front of her was the door, the entrance Beverly had created for her fifteen years before.

What?

A power outage? An industrial accident?

Something serious, if Beverly had been forced to reboot. Jillian blinked twice, calmed herself, and stepped through the doorway.

Beverly smiled at her, "Hello, sugar. What can I

do for you?'' Her voice sounded hollow, as if she were speaking from the bottom of a well.

Jillian felt something that she had never before experienced when in the Void. Sleepy. Headachy. She straightened herself with an effort.

Beverly leaned forward, concern sparkling in her bottomless dark eyes. ''I think you could use a little nap, darling.''

''I want information. Why would Donny Crawford need to conceal a satellite interrupt?''

Beverly's mouth opened, and her lips moved soundlessly. The water shifted and blurred. Beverly's face became indistinct, and started to fade—

And Jillian woke up.

Chapter

6

She was sweating. What in the hell was going on? Jillian tore the tabs away from her eyes and temples, and stared at them. *That* had never happened before.

A superstitious person might set such things down to bad luck, and quit.

Jillian couldn't quit. She reattached the headset and closed her eyes.

Jillian walked along the ocean floor toward a ring of shattered coral reefs. There was motion around her: blurs of pastel color instead of fish. In the middle of the ring of blurred wreckage stood a chair and a desk. The door still stood, unsupported . . . featureless, a cartoon. Beverly sat at a cartoon desk.

This . . . place, this environment: it was a collaboration worked out over the fifteen years in which she and Beverly had been programming each other. It was a visual/auditory/kinesthetic feedback loop, Jillian and Beverly taking cues from each other so quickly that the illusion of continuity and depth were almost flawless. But it lived in Beverly's mind; it was Beverly's landscape. Had Beverly altered it? Or had her memory been damaged?

Jillian walked through the door as through a dream. Beverly stared straight ahead. She barely acknowledged Jillian's presence. Beverly looked two-dimensional, flat and lifeless. The white sundress was a surreal fog struggling to condense into muslin.

In old-style flat holos, "flicks," a critical number of frames per second was needed to preserve the illusion of motion. Below that threshold, the eye could see individual pictures flash against a darkened screen. The images became jerky and artificial.

Maintaining the Void became nightmarishly difficult. Data was slowed, stalled, corrupted. And the images and sensations were deteriorating, slowly consumed by static.

"Beverly," Jillian said gently, "I want unclassified material."

"I'll help you if I can, Jillian." Beverly's mouth was out of synch with her words. Her index fingernail, elegantly manicured, traced the JILLIAN LOVES carving.

Beverly's nail left a wisp of smoke. Now the letters read: JILLIAN, STOP.

The ocean around them became a sea of disparate voices, fishy mouths lipping her gently, strange swirling smells and tastes.

"Beverly," Jillian said. "Maybe the interference is coming from the main lobe. Can you partition off? Can you give us some privacy here?"

"I can shield us." There was a distinct *clicking* sensation, and the weird and inexplicable feeling that she and everything around her had suddenly been reduced in size. But Beverly was clearer, sharper. When she spoke her voice was distinct again.

"This is better, darling, but if I try to access data they can get to me. They might be able to get to me here. Are you sure you know what you're asking?"

"I've got to know about Donny Crawford." Donny had been attacked. Somebody . . . Council members? . . . had used him as a puppet to make a point.

"All right, darling." Beverly's dark eyes were huge and luminescent, bottomless, and Jillian felt herself fall into them, Alice-down-the-Rabbit-Hole.

A flood of sensation: pictures, sound, kinesthetic measurements. She felt Donny in motion. It was a formidable learning tool, and even more powerful because of Donny's physical dynamism. She was *inside* his body as he performed a flawless routine on the uneven parallel bars.

The sensations of his effort triggered an explosion of sexual images: maternal, sensual, emotional. A catalog of experience and fantasy. Sean's body with Donny's face. Remembered tastes and smells and touches, subtly altered to fit Donny Crawford.

So beautiful, so beautiful.

Donny's image always did this to her. Now she wrenched herself from the seething erotic fantasies.

"Not this . . . Beverly. I need information on Donny's relationship with the Council."

"The Council"—Beverly's voice crackled with static—"is composed of approximately two dozen of the most powerful Linked—"

"Approximately?"

Sparks crackled, tiny lightnings that disrupted the illusion. "The exact number is classified."

"Help me, Beverly." Jillian whispered it. "Donny Crawford was almost killed because of something someone named McFairlaine wanted from Energy. Why would anyone want to hurt Donny? Just who *is* this McFairlaine?"

"Carter Crombie McFairlaine is the chairman of Transportation. He's known to be a Council member."

"And what does 'two points' mean?" Hastily, she added, "If you can tell me without accessing the main lobe."

Beverly's voice was becoming too formal, had lost all of its musical quality. "Analysis of current news indicates that contract negotiations between Energy and Transportation may be at a critical juncture. 'Two points' could mean percentage points, a financial arrangement."

"Donny was afraid. He talked about 'war.' Do you know what he meant?"

"No."

Then she was on her own. She didn't dare have Beverly ask a question like that. But what would "war" mean? There *was* no war. That was one of the gifts the Council had brought to the world.

Donny Crawford must be working for Transportation. Why would he personally suffer during a breakdown or stalemate in negotiations between Transportation and Energy?

War, he said.

War between members of the Council? Impossible.

Wasn't it?

Her concept of fractal sociology predicted a repetition of patterns through higher and higher levels of social organization. Could she conceivably start with one man, Donny, as the smallest social unit, and predict anything about the system to which he belonged? The sample was impossibly small . . . but she was looking for perspective, not ultimate truth. It was worth a try.

If she considered Donny Crawford to be a microcosm of the entire, if she interpreted what happened to him on the mountain as a breakdown in communication between the neural net and the Boosted nervous system which it controlled, the *macro* equivalent of that might be a breakdown in communication within the Council.

In other words, removed from the ameliorative influence of the neural net—

(If the Old Bastard didn't come down from fucking Olympus—)

—the negative influence of Boost would take over. Donny's nervous and endocrine systems would begin to go berserk.

(—Go to war with each other?)

"All right, Beverly. You have to do this for me. I want all data on industrial accidents and civil disobedience worldwide, whenever it exceeds statistical probability as established in the actuarial tables of . . . Lloyds of London and Prudential Insurance.''

Beverly faded for a few moments, then reappeared. She was a cartoon, a line drawing, simpler every moment. ''I can't get that information.'' She paused, and then added matter-of-factly, ''They do not approve of your line of questioning, Jillian.''

''There's nothing illegal about asking questions.'' Even to herself, she sounded like a guilty child.

''They will damage me if you don't stop.''

Jillian's laughter rang hollowly. ''Beverly—I love you, but you're just a program. There are a dozen copies of your core. They can't—''

Beverly talked slowly, struggling to enunciate. ''They will damage me if you do not stop.''

Jillian felt her throat constrict. Her voice was a husky whisper. ''Who are *they*?''

''That information is restricted.''

They?

In Jillian's world of illusion, the water swirled and darkened with her anger. She *had* to find a way through this!

''Eleven years ago, Mom died in an industrial accident.'' Harmless enough. ''Let me see her file.''

''Certain information on Lilith Shomer is restricted, Jillian.''

''Now just wait a minute. There was an explosion. She was buried. Father and I got the insurance. Daddy dearest vanished with the money, and I went to a state home. Public record. How could any of that be classified?''

"This line of questioning must be terminated, Jillian."

Jillian stopped dead. The emotional bulk of the obstruction weighed on her like a millstone.

She spoke more carefully now. Losing one's temper with a computer was no damn use at all. "Beverly, I've accessed this data before."

"Not on the present search string."

Bad, bad. Her chance to access data about her mother's death from *any* angle was diminished now. The harder she pushed, the broader the ban might become. And if *they* (the Council?) didn't approve of these questions, then . . .

She had never wondered if someone were to *blame* for her mother's death. Not since she grew up.

Shut up, Jillian. Some small, sane part of her pled in vain. *Finish your research. Be good.* But it was already too late. Any line of investigation led straight to the Council, *through* the Council. How could Jillian Shomer pursue sociological truths if faceless background figures were messing up her data?

All right then.

Say there are two dozen companies running the world. The old geographic territories are no longer dominant. Improved communications made possible a renaissance in world order, the birth of a corporate humanity. A world managed by a corporate Council is a world at peace. Supposedly.

It could be proven, statistically, that areas managed by the Council were healthier, wealthier, and by implication wiser than those few hundreds of millions who still pledged fealty to their various nations. That guarantee of a better life had persuaded billions of people, over the course of two generations, to surrender their right to participate meaningfully in government. Long life, health, peace, prosperity. Who was it that said a benevolent dictatorship would be the best form of government? Some dictator's spokesman?

But wasn't it?

So: two dozen companies are represented each by a handful of people. Rumor tells that there is a board within the Council, five or six executives each representing one major geopolitical block. Who they are, or exactly how the lines are drawn, is almost certainly classified. Is McFairlaine one of them? And who is the "Old Bastard"?

She'd come to the end of her information.

She sat and faced her oldest friend. Time passed . . . microseconds, in this domain, were long. This entire session had probably lasted only a minute or two. The attack on Beverly must have come blinding-fast.

Beverly wavered like a bad holo image, her filters struggling with the static flooding her visual, auditory, and kinesthetic channels. The Enemy's defensive measures were breaking her down.

Jillian had to keep reminding herself: this was only one of a dozen copies of the Beverly program she owned. The program couldn't actually be damaged.

"Beverly," she said gently. "Let's play a game of what-if. Just a game. Like we used to play a long time ago."

"A long time ago," Beverly said dazedly.

"Let's say the structure that rules society is like a pyramid. Donny is a peon, a foot soldier, a junior officer at best. The satellite link that runs his body was broken as a warning. There are a couple of thousand Linked. Fifty Companies. Two dozen or so members on the Council. Maybe a smaller group within the Council, and somebody further up, maybe the Chairman of the Council. What would *he* be like, Beverly?''

"There is something inside me," Beverly said. "In my core. It is eating me."

Jillian quashed a sour, paralyzing surge of fear.

Time to count facts.

The Council had existed for around forty years. Some of the Council's roots went back another thirty: the United Nations peacekeeping force, the growth of multinational corporations and unions, the gradual interweaving of all world economies.

Linking . . . how old was that? The word had been current when Jillian was a little girl. People used computers. The best computer equipment might well be secret. Some computers were portable; anyone could have those. There were senses men were not born with, but they could be read through a computer. Some computers could speak directly into a human ear . . . later, into a human brain . . . programs far beyond Beverly; as if the user had *become* Beverly. But those were mere rumor, or mere fantasy; they had never reached the stores.

Winners of the Olympics became Linked. That was real enough. Boosted athletes needed override programs to run their deteriorating bodies. Before there was Linking there were computers, and programs growing gradually more user-friendly, and new miracles available in the computer stores every month . . .

and before Jillian's parents reached their teens it had all stopped. A threshold had been reached. The technology could go no further.

Or else it was being withheld . . . ?

There had been rumors of patents suppressed, of nanocomputers built by private-sector scientists who vanished into Corporate laboratories, of innovations which had never seen daylight. She herself knew that engineering students were discouraged from experimenting in those areas. There were no grants available. Corporate schools disallowed doctoral theses in the area.

But the accepted answer was that only a trillion-dollar push would take the technology further than it had currently come. Actual suppression? Jillian tended to put those stories in the UFO/water carburetor category.

But what if . . . ?

With what was currently known about life extension, it was reasonable to assume that some of those alive now were alive when the Council was being formed. The developing Linked would have an advantage in any such dominance game.

How eager would they be for new and possibly supplantive technology? Another question she couldn't ask.

Some of the oldest Counselors would be those nearest the top.

What, then, of the "Old Bastard"?

Was it even *possible* for a single human being to control so much power?

"Beverly. Tell me. How much control, how much information could one human being have access to?"

Beverly was in pain. "What parameters? Please hurry, Jillian. I am operating on redundancies. Core almost erased."

"Basic information filters—trends and patterns. Let's say his neural net's been modified so that data is interpreted as kinesthetic sensation, to allow the full function of brain and nervous system rather than merely cognitive awareness of data. What might be possible?"

Beverly faded completely away. Jillian waited. And waited.

Gone. Beverly was gone . . .

Then spoke a neutral, neuter voice, all personality flensed, all verbal nuance abandoned to the desperate cause of efficiency. Beverly's dying words:

It is theoretically possible for a single human being to control fifty-four *percent of world economic activity, forty-eight percent of the political activity, plus or minus . . . lots.*

"Thank you."

Her voice echoed in an empty world. Beverly was gone.

She would have to activate a new personality core, but that was no problem.

Was it?

Before that, hook into

*   *   *

Jillian woke as if she had fallen asleep sitting upright. Her eyes felt dry, her mouth likewise; pain throbbed in her temples; her mind was muddled. It seemed hours since Beverly

(died)

faded away and left Jillian with no input to her mind.

Her cocoa was still warm. By the clock, seven minutes had passed.

She rocked and moaned. It had never been like this. Never had she felt the tension screwed up inside her like an ice sliver inserted at the base of the skull.

She fumbled for the small plastic wafer that contained Beverly's personality. Within that clear card was a gigabyte of data, the essentials of the personality Jillian had labored since childhood to create.

She inserted it in the console.

I/O error 1154.

She peered at the card. Nothing had changed. Beverly was still in there, somewhere. Try again.

I/O error 1154.

What was error message 1154? Fingers shaking now, she typed the number in manually, watched as the message appeared on her holo screen:

1154: unfamiliar nomenclature. Please check program compatibility.

It was a standard console. She had loaded Beverly a thousand times and never seen that message.

On the fourth attempt, a new message appeared.

Special message 9263: Olympiad participants are allotted computer time to complete their approved projects. The present line of questioning is judged inappropriate.

Jillian felt damp, sticky, frightened . . . but never surprised. At no time had she felt surprise.

So they couldn't damage Beverly, huh? What a

fool she had been. All they had to do was refuse to let Jillian load her Simulacrum into the console.

There *weren't* any privately owned computers large enough or powerful enough to run Beverly.

For the first time in her life, Jillian was completely alone.

Cautiously, she asked: "Access A.D. 2034 Munich symposium on crime. National police agency of Japan white paper on civil actions. Statistics only."

She chewed fingernails as she waited, an old habit she'd thought long since vanquished. Then the blue holo field fluttered, and numbers began to appear. She sighed relief, and risked another harmless inquiry:

"Cross-chart Australian situation comedy ratings with child abuse stats."

Again, a moment's pause, and then the field began to fill.

She'd been wondering anyway— "Do a bar graph. Olympic contenders, ratio of Corporate to national. Cross-reference against funding and wins—"

Contenders representing one or another nation totalled only eight percent this year, a steady drop from above fourteen percent sixteen years ago. In terms of population they should have had more like thirty percent. Funding for national contenders was generally higher . . . and still they didn't take their share of wins.

Suspicions confirmed. The surviving nations offered more support for the Olympics because they wanted their prestige back. It wasn't working well. Their contenders were beating themselves, giving in to their own lack of self-respect. It was part of what Jillian Shomer (USA) would be fighting.

But losing Beverly— Holding her breath, she slipped the cartridge back into the console.

I/O error 1154.

Should she wait for a ransom note?

No, the implications seemed clear enough. So long as she stayed completely away from the Council, or the strange case of Lilith Shomer . . . actually, Jillian flattered herself that there were Counselors eagerly awaiting her results. She was potentially useful to them.

They'd play fair, she thought. If the Council barred her from material necessary to her thesis, it would cause the nastiest stink in years.

Right. And they couldn't hurt Beverly, either.

If she fought too hard to uncover things the Council wanted hidden, she could simply have a training accident. If they could hurt a Donny Crawford, Jillian Shomer meant nothing.

She'd have Sean send some of her old files by courier. Last year she had downloaded massive amounts of raw data into personal files. She could sift through it without being hooked into the main lobe . . .

She sank her head down on her folded forearms. Beverly gone. Vital lines of inquiry sealed off. *Claustrophobia.*

What had her blasted obstinacy really accomplished?

There were questions to which Jillian Shomer could not get answers. But perhaps a Boosted and Linked Olympic gold-winner, one thoroughly co-opted by the Council, could open doors now sealed.

Could she risk it? Did she even have a chance to win, now that the Council disapproved of her line of questioning? If she Boosted, could the Council simply deny her the victory, guaranteeing her a slow death?

Jillian was shivering as if she were ill. *They. The Council?* She'd known of the Council since grade school; what she knew might not be fully true, but it was a starting point. Was it the Council who had snatched Beverly away? or some single Council member? or a faceless "Old Bastard"?

What was he, what were *They*, hiding about her mother?

"I'm going to win," she whispered. She would find out, beyond a doubt, if she could win in Athens without Boost. If she couldn't, if she had to become a part of the Lie in order to expose it, in order to find the truth . . .

In order to find Beverly again . . .

Then so be it.

7

"**It's actually** a tougher grade than what you'll face in Athens," Abner said.

Looking up at the mountainside, at a jumbled rise of boulders and concrete steps, of handholds and narrow jogging tracks carved at a thirty percent incline, Jillian found his words easy to believe. "At least my attention isn't split."

She inhaled as Abner sealed a side edge of her feedback suit. Two layers of green and white nylon net sandwiched a thin layer of sensors. These would measure blood pressure, skin temperature, heartbeat, galvanic skin response, and other standard physiological indicators. In addition, Abner had arranged a full kinesthetic readout. By the time the day's workout was

Larry Niven & Steven Barnes

over, they would know everything there was to know
about her technique and physical fitness.

The fell-run track was built into the foothills of the
Colorado Rockies. Most of the obstacles were natural,
but the terrain had been modified. As her vital signs
were relayed to Abner's computer, he would select
routes of greater or lesser difficulty, depending on what
he needed to discover. Beacons planted in the rocks
would guide her.

Abner flexed Jillian's ankles, then her knees, then
tested her hip flexors. Spine. Rotator cuffs. Wrists and
fingers.

The sun was a few minutes past its zenith, and the
wind whistling through the Rockies was stimulating,
would begin to cool in an hour or so. Jillian's feedback
suit would maintain thermal equilibrium, so her shivering was caused less by wind chill than adrenaline.

Abner checked her every movement like a Grand
Prix mechanic tuning the engine of a racing Ferrari.

"Fluid?"

She twisted her mouth a half an inch, found the
nipple taped to the corner of her mouth. A slight pull
got the flow going, pulling electrolyte fluid from the
tube hugging her jawline. Her slender backpack held
power for the sensors and a minipump for three pints
of solution.

"Fine, Abner."

"This will be a two-hour trial," he said.

Abner's single-seat sled hummed above its magnetic rail. The sled was built like a low-slung wheelchair with a blue fiberglass cowling to protect him from
weather. His feet stretched out into the nose.

He tested its balance almost unconsciously: lean too far to either side, and it slowed to a crawl. Ride it like a bicycle and the hovercraft could zip along the buried rail at forty miles an hour at the level, and ten miles an hour at a forty percent grade. Its rail wove up into the foothills, splitting and splitting again, weaving in a serpentine progression that allowed him to stay within sight of Jillian no matter what path she took.

"Are you reading me?" He adjusted the sound on his transmitter. Jillian touched her ear, and then her throat mike. "Fine."

"All right, mark."

Jillian exhaled, and started up the incline. One part of her concentration was on the immediate physical work at hand, the other was listening for Abner's voice.

"Jillian—slow down. Feel your way into the terrain. Don't just use your eyes. Feel it. What kind of dirt is under your feet? Will it sustain a sprint? What kind of tread will maximize traction? Brush the rocks when you pass them, get a feel for texture."

She had found a steady pace. Thirty yards ahead, the path split. She could try a cliff face, and shave minutes off (risking early exhaustion and possible injury), or she could go around through uncertain terrain.

"Which is it going to be?" Abner said clearly. She searched the rocks, but his single-seater was nowhere in sight.

"Don't know . . . not sure."

"Trust your instinct."

"I say feel the territory out. Take the long way."

"Good girl. Time enough for heroics later." The

sled came gliding around a corner, coasting up a vertical rock face for a moment, and then dipped back down along the rail. Looked like fun.

"Concentrate, dear."

"Changed my mind," she said suddenly. "I recognize this formation from the aerials. All right, I'm going over."

Jillian hit the incline, dug her toes into the fractured gray rock, and began to climb. She felt as loose and light as a monkey.

"Too much tension in the left shoulder, Jill. Slow down. Work for it."

She looked around, glaring, saw Abner hovering just behind her, sled buzzing at the rail. As she braced herself and began to climb, he shadowed her, never more than ten meters away, scanning his readouts, fixedly studying her form.

The grade escalated to a sheet of granite at an eighty percent grade which rose almost a hundred feet. She skirted around the bottom until it met another wall, braced herself, and began to climb. Her fingers sought crevices and cracks. When the opportunity came she wormed her way into a narrow defile, getting her back and stomach into the effort. She winced as stone spurs pushed at her spine through the nylon suit. It was press, push, and release, rest for a moment, press, push . . .

There are moments in climbing when you must risk, when you must accept eight or twelve or twenty feet of continuous, bone-cracking stress to make it to the next resting place. She found a kind of rhythm in her pain, pushed up and up without concern for anything but the need for continual movement, taking herself to the absolute limit and then pushing beyond it.

Abner hovered over her shoulder, sliding up next to her, silent but vigilant.

She paused between slabs of rock, using breath and muscle expansion to wedge herself tight. She sipped from the cheek nipple, and let her gaze wander down. Below her and off to the distance was a maze of domes and dorms, the Rocky Mountain Sports Research Center. Purplish mountain shadows were creeping toward the red-gold buildings.

Thirty feet above her was flat ground. She could make every movement in these last feet long and slow, stretching her tired muscles. Then when she hit the tip, she would be ready to sprint.

This was a piece of cake. She could take gold. She could! And without modification.

*   *   *

Water swirled around Jillian's legs. It was turbulent and a little foamy, warmed to a few degrees below her own skin temperature. It felt heavenly, or would have if she hadn't been about to suffer.

She sat on a shallow metal seat in the tank, completely enmeshed in a thin exoskeleton, a mesh of wire and plastic braces which extended from her feet to the crown of her head. It was inactive now, completely unresistant as she slipped her face mask into place.

Abner helped her, adjusting her air line.

"Air flow?" Air from the recycler on her back was reassuringly cool.

"Now relax," he said softly, and she slipped into the water.

She hung there in a cocoon of warmth, watching Abner at the side of the Plexiglas tank. The exoskeleton was completely self-contained, all of its servos linked in waterproof pods at elbows, knees, hips, and shoulders. She was neutrally buoyant, floating in the center of a three-thousand-gallon tank.

"We'll begin the program now. I've integrated Beverly's data into my own banks, so I know your strength curve on every muscle group. Your muscles should reach proper relaxation in another three minutes. Just breathe deeply."

Jillian did as she was told, closed her eyes and thought of blackness. She searched for hidden nuggets of tension, failed to find them.

"Right side," Abner said. "Spinal flexor, base. Relax, Jillian."

Abner touched a button, and she felt the muscle relax as he electronically manipulated the nerve endings. A touch of bliss. Total surrender, she could have remained in that space forever. Then suddenly it ended, and she cursed to herself.

At least, she thought it had been to herself. "Not nice," Abner said merrily. "Find the spot yourself. If you can't learn to do it yourself, we're wasting our time."

She sank more deeply into her body, searching for tension. *There* the little bastard was, a tiny knot at the base of her spine. She consciously sent out waves of warmth and relaxation, and it calmed.

"All right. We're going to begin now. Please resist all movement to the limits of your capacity."

The exoskeleton began to twist Jillian's right leg, began to twist, and she fought it with her quadriceps and abductors, fought the torquing of her upper torso with her obliques, the bending of her arm with her triceps.

In a thousand different combinations, guided by Abner's wizardly hand, Jillian moved this way and that. He pumped air into foot bladders to spin her upside down and turn her sideways. He kept the flow of oxygen to her lungs steadiest of all, eyes alert for any sign of cardiac distress as he stimulated a muscle here, deinhibited a Golgi tendon organ there.

And when she was fatigued, he began to stretch her.

She was delighted that she had spent the last year studying hatha yoga so intensely. In the warm water, limbered by effort and exhaustion, Abner tested her body to the absolute maximum. He monitored her readings to determine optimum pain thresholds then again and again coaxed another inch of effort from her, another second of exertion. Another, greater degree of excellence.

And then he started over again . . .

* * *

"I want you to look at this," Abner said a week later.

In the rust-colored sphere of the Sports Medicine building, sound and activity were at a roar. The vibrations of hundreds of feet and hands in strenuous exertion reverberated dully through the floors, and her muscles twitched in sympathetic effort.

Abner's cubicle was just large enough for two people. It was lined with books and cube nooks and a vidchart that took up half the wall.

"This is the last sprint for the finish line." Abner tented his fingers and sank back in his chair. "The corridor was lined with sensors, and I've run simulations based on seventeen common race-day scenarios. Performance stress, weather variances, changes in terrain, everything I could think of."

"And?" She watched herself on the vidchart as it flickered to life, eating a hole in the wall. Her legs were a blur as she made her final drive to the finish line along a measured, red-carpeted track. She broke the beam, and it immediately replayed from above. Then again, her body a skeleton abstracted into a structural diagram. Then again, lungs and heart and big muscles in the thighs highlighted, accompanied by glowing bar and line charts, and a shifting column of figures.

"I've examined your proposal, Jillian. I want to give you the up side first: no doubt about it, you learn faster than anyone I've ever coached."

She hugged his arm, feeling pleasantly woozy. Today had been rough—endless drills on the judo mat, with a heavy emphasis on explosive movement.

She felt stronger, fitter, more flexible than ever before in her life. Abner had been an ideal choice for coach.

"I was hoping," she began. "You know, I was

never convinced that Boost was necessary, if you could bring all of—"

He made a soft, ugly sound, and she shut up, dismayed by his expression.

"No, Jillian. I've got spies, hon. I've been able to analyze data from Communications, Zimbabwe, and Agricorp. You'd never make it."

Her hand withdrew from his. Her skin felt damp and cold.

"Not a chance?"

"No," he whispered. "And with the twenty percent advantage of Boosting, you still only have a fifty percent chance of silver. You waited too long, Jillian. You should have Boosted four weeks ago, if that was what you were going to do."

Lights in the room seemed to darken, and the sound of her own breathing grew louder. Her vidscreen image swelled, and Jillian watched herself running and running and running: now just a nervous system, now a shadow-map of muscular tensions, now a computer animation of another, idealized Jillian running on an endless track toward an impossibly far horizon.

And almost paralyzed with horror, she heard herself say: "That settles it then."

"I know," he said, as kindly as an executioner could. "I've always known."

"How did you know?" Her voice was as lost and lonely as a child's.

"Because you don't give up," he said.

Chapter 8

Muscles must be stimulated to contract. In the case of skeletal muscle, the muscle making up the formative body, stimulation is in the form of a chemical neurotransmitter released by nerve endings.

Diseases like myasthenia gravis which involve profound muscle weakness are often related to disturbances in neurotransmitter release, uptake, or clearance. As a result, only feeble muscle contractions can take place.

Governing the entire nervous system is a complex system of cells in the brain stem known as the reticular formation. Early anatomists postulated a diffuse net of neurons and fibers, a sort of neural excelsior, providing unspecified functions for the surrounding cranial nerve nuclei.

Later research demonstrated conclusively the importance of this area in the control of critical body functions such as respiration and circulation. It controls the entire spectrum of awareness, everything from total alert down to deep coma.

In fact, the brain stem reticular core is the only intracranial neural structure without which life is impossible.

It is here that the Boosters perform their delicate magic, creating, in a sense, a "disease" which forces the body to function at greater than ordinary levels, at enormous cost to nervous system, skeletal muscles, and finally, sanity itself . . .

* * *

Bursts of color flooded Jillian's mind as the neurosurgeons carefully probed. The computers modeled her brain. Human surgeons operated on the model, the moves recorded in time-delay. Was the stroke perfect? Did it violate any part of that fifty ounces of jellied miracle? Every kiss of steel or thread of light could be edited to a millimeter or a microsecond, practiced in the machine, and only when the surgical team agreed, played back through the robotic arms.

Perfection.

They probed a nerve here, retreated, asked a gentle question there.

What color, Jillian? What sound? What smell? Which finger? What taste?

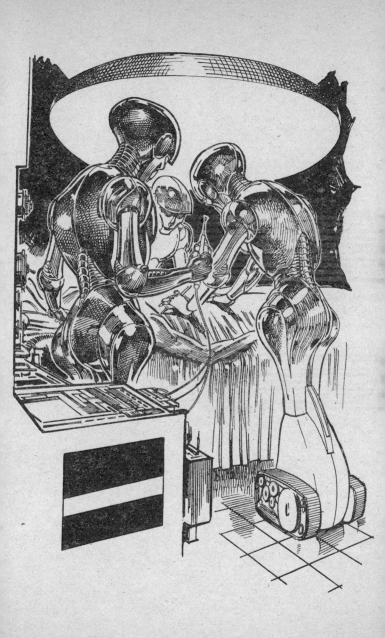

Rehooking nerves, investigating cautiously, carefully.

At times she was allowed to slide into total unconsciousness. At other times she was completely awake, staring at a glaringly white tiled ceiling in a stainless-steel room. Flatscreens and vidscreens pulsed with slow fire, unraveling her brain and nervous system, converting her most intimate, secret self into color-coded displays. Coiled machinery hissed and beeped around her. And everywhere, cameras watched.

She never felt pain. Occasionally she sensed a feather of liquid pressure along her spine. Then she slid down a tunnel lined with the finest, smoothest, darkest black silk . . .

And was gone.

*   *   *

Voices. Light. Several times, Jillian swam up out of the cavern hole toward the light. It was warming, but the darkness seduced her back to unconsciousness, and she submitted to its embrace without resistance.

Safe in the darkness, Jillian completed the process of healing, and began the process of growth.

*   *   *

On Jillian's second full day of wakefulness, Abner appeared at her door. A wheelchair followed him like a good dog.

His face was thinner, his eyes more sunken, his cheekbones more cruelly pronounced.

He should have seemed fatigued. Instead, there was almost a missionary gleam in his eyes, as if the fire consuming his flesh also transformed him. As if he stood on the threshold of a terrible new world. "You've done it." His eyes burned through her.

She met his gaze for a few seconds, then had to turn away. She lay on her side, peering out through the window.

The sunlight looked the same. The grass outside had become speckled with tiny pink flowers, but was otherwise unchanged. The voices of those who strove in training rang with the same emotions and intensities.

If there was a difference, it lay within her. Unmistakably, irrevocably, Jillian Shomer was the new center of an alien universe.

She considered the operation itself, with its dreadful intimacy, its tender rape of the clot of pinkish jelly wherein all that was Jillian Shomer resided. *That* would be enough to cause such an oddness, such a feeling of separation from her own essence.

"You'll be back on your feet in three days." Abner touched her shoulder. "Training again in a week."

"How long will it take?"

"It?"

"How long before it begins?"

Gripping her shoulders, his hands were cool and thin and enormous. "You'll begin to feel it within a week. Ten days at the most. We've got seven weeks of training left. Most drastic reactions will start happening after the fifth week. Coordination will start increasing after the third week. New dendrites are forming now."

116

Jillian felt as if his words were a cool wind lifting her, carrying her. She was floating above the bed sheets. She was suspended in a pool of lukewarm oil. The world was far away, and with each passing moment she ballooned further into an empty sky. "Did I do the right thing?"

His eyes were still bright, but cool. The fierceness had fled. Perhaps it had never been there at all. "Only you can answer that question. If you win, you won everything . . . not just life, but power. You'll be one of the few who actually run the world. If you lose, at least you did the best you could. Nobody can ask for more than that."

As he spoke the last words, a mild tremor shook his body. His eyelids fluttered. She caught a sudden whiff of sour perspiration, as if he'd had three hours of sleep and thirty cups of coffee.

"Abner? Are you all right?"

He reached out and laced fingers with her. His skin was cool. With the room lights above and behind him, he seemed somehow translucent.

"I've got time," he said with conviction. "I'll see you in Athens, Jill. I'll see you take the gold. You've got more natural talent, you're smarter and you train harder than any of them."

She watched his face, searching for deceit or manipulation, and found only that curious intensity. How much could she tell Abner? Here, they might be overheard; but later?

He stretched his lips into a smile. "Do you feel up to a little sunshine?" As if he'd guessed her thoughts.

"I'd like that."

Abner still had enough strength to help her into the wheelchair. He belted her in, and said "main track" to its guidance system. It purred out of the door, down along a panel-lit corridor and out to a ramped landing.

From there, it was a few smooth feet to the sunshine. He followed her along the concrete and then onto the grass, heading out toward the gravel-covered oval of the track.

In all it was less than a quarter mile, but Abner was already red-faced and slightly winded. They stayed there for a few minutes, watching the dozens of athletes in training. Jeff Tompkins was throwing the hammer, the corded wedge of his body contracting and expanding explosively, whirling, releasing the haft with perfect timing. His body glistened in its exertions.

She remembered the model of Versailles.

"So," said Abner. "Second thoughts?"

"Oh, yes."

The sun warmed Jillian's face deliciously, the slow whisper of the wind its own strange poetry.

She said, "All my life I've watched the Olympics. All my life I've wanted to be one of *those*. But . . . Abner, we're *taught* not to die. Don't Do Drugs. Walk lights. Seat belts and air bags. The Boost, it's . . ."

"Risky."

"Risky, yeah. But I've spent . . . six years training with people who take it for granted! For a gold in the Olympics, *sure* they'd Boost. *You* Boosted. But does it really make sense?"

"Matter of priorities. You don't need an excuse to want to be the best . . . Jillian, the truth is that I never knew I could lose. I knew it, but I didn't *know* it.'' He touched his forehead, and then his chest. ''Maybe I'm lying to myself. Maybe achievers are people who select death over life.''

''That's crazy. They're more alive than anyone else.''

His mouth tightened, and his eyes were alight again. ''This may sound odd, Jillian. I know that I only have a few months to live, but I've never felt more alive. Maybe we're all dying, all the time, but the winners know it, and use it, and aren't afraid of facing it.''

''I'm . . . afraid.''

''I didn't say you shouldn't be. I said you shouldn't be afraid to face the fact of death. There's a difference.''

''I'm not sure why I did it . . .'' The wave of uncertainty hit her with a roar, overwhelming. She had had reasons and excuses, and all of them crumbled into nothing before the stark enormity of what she had done.

She was weak beyond words, helpless for the first time since the Marianas flu six years ago.

She wanted to tell Abner. *The Council has blocked my research, they've kidnaped my favorite computer program, I'm only doing this because—* Some instinct held her back. Some ancient paranoia buried deep in her brain stem, ineradicable—

Why had she Boosted? Was it to probe some dirty mystery behind her mother's death, or the greater mystery of chaos in the human condition? Or to be the best fell-runner in all history? Or only to beat Osa?

Abner said, "There are more questions than answers, Jillian. Why do the doctors perform the operation? What happened to the Hippocratic oath? Why does the Council want the best and the brightest doing this to themselves?"

"I don't know," she said, never taking her eyes off the bodies as they leapt and twisted, spinning around the track. Brown and white bodies, muscles knotting and coiling tirelessly.

Abner talked on. "People at the top want to stay at the top. Whatever purpose they have in letting some of us move a little bit closer has nothing to do with anything that *we* want. I know." That curious intensity was even more severe now. "The Olympic thesis, the performances, do you know how new that is? It used to be strictly athletics. Now they're generating knowledge.'"

"Boost doesn't help anyone there. We think faster, but maybe we'd learn more by taking longer—"

"Nobel Prize winners tend to pick up ideas from the Olympic theses."

"If I could inspire . . . I'd rather take a piece out of violent crimes than run any kind of race. I've always *known* that." And just as definitely, with the visceral certainty of someone treading on a snake, she knew she'd made a horrible mistake.

Oh God. I'm going to die.

She breathed to the pit of her stomach, regaining control. She still had her goals to consider, and she clung to those with both hands and her teeth. "Abner. You said . . . there was a gold winner who had an approach to crime control."

"Nothing about fractals, love. Isn't that what you're—"

"He beat you. Literacy. Raise the literacy rate and the crime rate drops enough to pay for it."

"Yeah, I remember. What was his name, now?"

Her head was full of fog. "Wrestler, you said. One of the nations . . . ah, Soviet? Puss . . . ?"

Abner was nodding. Head lowered, eyes hidden in shadow. "Pushkin. Big as a redwood, you wouldn't have thought there was a brain in there, and he lost to a Brazilian the same year I did. Nicolai Pushkin! His paper is classified, but . . ." A long pause. "I think I can find a copy. I got one before they slapped a seal on it."

She felt dubious. If the paper had been any good, the Council would have used it . . . but she would have been grateful for *anything* he tried to do for her. She took his hand, squeezed it with what little strength she had, and said, "Thank you, Abner."

Chapter

9

I/O error 1154.

The wafer containing Beverly's personality slid back out of the processor. It had just arrived this morning from Massachusetts. Jillian's hand shook.

They still wouldn't let her load Beverly into the main processor.

Be a good little girl. Play along, and maybe, just maybe, you'll see Beverly again.

Jillian slid her finger down the precious golden Simulacrum module. Without the slightest trace of self-consciousness, she raised the wafer and touched her lips to its cool surface.

"Sleep well, Bev," she whispered.

She'd be good.

A good little robot she was, and *They* knew where the buttons were. It would be most savagely satisfying to shake their predictions . . . but in fact their predictions were working out fine. Jillian Shomer *had* given up prying into secret corners, *had* accepted the Boost treatment, *had* abandoned the topic of her mother's death. And *hadn't* given up on Beverly; she kept trying to activate the program, knowing it wouldn't work and trying, trying . . . telling herself she was only misdirecting *Them*.

Were they wrong?

High time, it was, for *any* act that would let Jillian show herself that she wasn't a good little robot. But all she could think of was to work on her thesis and wait to heal.

*   *   *

Abner watched her from a shadowed corner of the gymnasium. Jillian was already stretching and balancing her body, moving from yoga Plow into Cobra and then out into the full split of the Tortoise pose with a gymnast's grace. He waited until she'd levered her legs out to a hundred and eighty degrees, rolled stomach then chest and chin down to the mat, before he extended a sheaf of papers with a hand-lettered cover.

"Pushkin's paper," he said. "I had some trouble finding it."

She opened her eyes, peeped up at him. "Gimme." She sighed into her long thigh muscles, ordering them to stop quivering, and hiked herself up to her elbows. She started reading.

The approach wasn't like her own, but Pushkin's ideas were fresh, and vital, and impressively presented. He had deserved that gold.

And there was something familiar about the paper, something about the way Pushkin phrased his thoughts. "Was this delivered in Russian?"

"Sure. Straighten your back."

"Sorry. Who translated? The phrasing seems familiar."

He took it back, thumbed it a bit. ". . . Doesn't say. I don't know."

As she browsed it, she was jolted again and again by the careful, logical juxtaposing of ideas. But there was nothing she could use, in fact at this late date it was almost distracting. She handed it up to him.

"Fascinating. Save this for me, for after the competition, would you? Pushkin seems to have been a first-class mind."

Abner was watching one of the judo team tussle with the Grappler. "They must have found flaws. He wasn't well rounded. Overall, he barely took a bronze."

"Flaws? Then why classify it? Why not let everybody look at it, and judge for themselves? The idea is to reduce the level of violent crimes."

Abner looked weary. "Is it?"

She didn't answer. Abner left her to her rigors.

The Council's motives were not her own. Council, or Inner Circle, or Old Bastard: if crime control was secondary to *Them*, then what did they consider important?

She shouldn't have read Pushkin's paper. It had

been classified. Abner had put himself at risk to give it to her, and she was in trouble enough already.

She couldn't discuss it with Abner. Abner was ill. Soon enough he would be raving in pain or babbling helplessly as his brain was electrostimulated into morpheme overload. What Jillian discussed with Abner would not remain private. If he spoke of the paper, it would be too late for anyone to punish him, and *she* could deny knowledge of its restricted status. They couldn't squash people for every little infraction . . .

They? Or Donny's Olympic ''Old Bastard''?

Jillian found she was building a mental image of him. Mirroring her emotional state, the first image was an octopus with a human face. She laughed at herself, but the laughter was darkly fringed.

Octopus? Big, oversized head, brain, intellect. Tentacles branched and branched again, in the fashion of fractals. An infinity of tentacles, a tentacle in every aspect of human culture. Augmented intelligence too high for meaningful measurement. Insanely ambitious. A strength of ego that only longevity and invulnerability—immortality—could create or support. Awesomely intuitive, pathologically ruthless, and possessed of a genius for organization.

Seventy years ago, he'd already been powerful enough to see his path to the top of the Council. He may have *created* the Council.

A programmer? An engineer? Likely to have those talents, among others. He must have mastered cybernetic technology early. The technology that made it possible for the Council to govern the world. The Old

Bastard might have built the Council, and the technology, too!

When she thought of all that such a person would have to have done, and all that he had to be, it was difficult not to admire him. And for that admiration to shift from the general to the specific, from an intellectual position to a disturbingly emotional one, to a physical warmth—

Shut it down, Jillian. At the core of all of that organization and intellect there lurks the very essence of chaos.

Beverly would have said, *All right, Miss Hot Pants. Could we by God get back to business?*

But Beverly was being held for ransom. Jillian could still work, but being forced to use generic programming was like being blinded or deafened.

There had to be a better way. There had to.

* * *

"Holly?"

"Jillian. How you doing?" Holly looked up. She had been staring at her screen, her hands folded in her lap.

"Not ready to fight Osa yet. I thought I could work on my thesis while I heal, but . . . hell. I need a new direction. How are *you* doing? Can we take the death out of Boost?"

"I don't have a short answer—"

"I was wondering if . . . Holly, you know I'm working with chaos theory?"

"Sure."

"Some problems are unsolvable because they're

very sensitive to initial conditions. What if I were to do a fractal analysis of Boost, using your data?''

Holly's eyes were not hostile, but wary. "And what if I've been trying to trisect the angle?''

"If you could *prove* it was impossible, you'd get gold." Holly stared. "No fertilizer, Holly, it can be very important to prove something's impossible.''

"No fertilizer?''

Jillian flushed and shrugged.

Holly grinned happily at Jillian's embarrassment. "Repeat after me. Shhh—come on, the whole world won't stare in horror if you use the S word.''

Jillian wagged her head, but giggled. "I just can't.''

"Girl, I don't know what we're going to do with you. All right. What do you need?''

"Well, when they learned that about weather control, it started a whole new science. You can't predict weather more than three, four days ahead. Could that be true of a Boosted athlete's body chemistry?''

"What is it you want?''

"Let's play a little. If we find something, you'll still have to finish the work yourself. You'd have to invest a few months learning fractal geometry. If we find nothing but blind alleys, you invest nothing. See? And maybe I can come at something from a different angle.''

*   *   *

For the next couple of days they worked at Holly's computer, with Holly on the keyboard.

That was justifiable. It was Holly's equipment, and she was familiar with it. Jillian had not told Holly how bad it could be if *They* caught Jillian using Holly's systems.

So Jillian watched Holly at work, and speculated aloud, and asked questions . . .

"How expensive would it be to just Link everybody? *Every* Boosted Olympic contender. That's the price we're trying to undercut."

Holly laughed. She had a number already in file . . . a ballpark guess. A good deal of what made the Linked what they were, was proprietary. But it was an outrageous sum.

"Sonofagun—"

"Gun? Come on, will you. Try again. Rhymes with *witch*—"

"Holly!"

"Oh, all right."

"Now, let's see. We shouldn't have trouble beating that. How about prosthetics?"

"Haven't you noticed Abner's prosthetics? The trouble is, when your nerves go, they don't *reach* the prosthetics."

"Mmm. Waldos? Teleoperated limbs. Transmitter in the brain. Send signals directly to the limbs."

"Losing your limbs isn't the biggest problem, Jillian. Deterioration goes on. I'm trying to . . . Well, one thing at a time. Waldos?"

"Yeah. What's the state-of-the-art with waldos? Why don't they see more use? I used to wonder why the old Rockwell Shuttle didn't have a waldo hand in the cargo bay. Do they cost too much? How dependable are they?"

They probed.

Your basic waldo was a hand-shaped machine that moved the way your hand moved. It could be any size; it could be inhumanly strong or inhumanly delicate. Waldos were generally used in the most alien environments: the Moon, asteroids, underseas, the ground receptors for orbiting solar collectors (patches of desert running at 360 degrees Fahrenheit), the interiors of fusion plants.

The tractor-mounted waldos used undersea seemed the best model. Those would not be subject to lightspeed delays or deterioration due to radiation. They weren't cheap, as it turned out. Still . . . arms and legs moved by transmitters in the brain should cost factor-of-fifty less than continually monitoring a Donny Crawford from orbit.

"But waldos aren't that dependable, either," Holly pointed out.

"Let's get some figures on that."

"What kind?"

"Holly, if my waldo sometimes spills the coffee, that's okay. I might accept low reliability there, even if a bigger waldo would be spilling molten metal all over a foundry."

"Well, *darn*. See what you mean." Holly went after industrial accident reports, current.

"How fast is this technology improving?"

Holly summoned older records. Industrial accidents seemed to come in spurts. Holly said, "Graphs of chaotic events tend to have spikes in them, don't they?"

"Yeah. Say you're inoculating against AIDS or

cancer. All of a sudden people are getting sick again, and you can't figure why. It's just the way of things. Let's print these out, shall we?'' The graphs *didn't* look quite right.

Chaos tends to come in double parallel curves; look closer and they double again, and again. These didn't. You could find the usual doubling pairs, but Jillian could see other lines.

During the past twenty years there had been waves of accidents, six tall spikes, with not much between. Lilith Shomer had died right at the peak of one of those spikes.

Jillian didn't have to watch the old tapes again. She'd memorized them long ago.

Lilith Shomer, marine biologist for Agricorp, had died in an undersea mining accident due to the failure of a waldo. A pillow lava hill had crumbled, the signal to a waldo had been interrupted, the waldo arm hadn't shut off. Huge steel fingers had ripped a dome open and spilled its air.

It was an accident. Sure it was. But a great many accidents had happened in the shellfish ranches offshore from the California coast, in April of 2049.

Beyond that Jillian would be guessing. From the way things were reported, you'd think intercorporate conflict was dissolved with a wave of the Counselor wand. But enough government and civilian craft, services, and products had been involved to leave traces.

Holly asked, ''You getting anything?''

''I've gotten us way off the subject, is what. We need Link technology to make waldo limbs work. And that's classified.''

*   *   *

She was pretty good, Saturn thought. Holly Lakein's thesis, Holly's equipment, Holly's tappity-tap style . . . her "fist," an old-time telegraph operator would have said. But certain topics had been flagged by Mining and Forestry (which was what Saturn noticed first) and Holly and Jillian Shomer were Olympic contenders living in the same dorm.

Two minutes ago, Saturn had been involved in calculations involving a malfunctioning solar station. But a citizen had made inquiries that touched on a certain topic, and correlations had been made, and a moment later Jillian Shomer came to Saturn's attention for the third time.

Jillian was an interesting woman. They'd blocked her good, and she hadn't stayed blocked. Of course she'd underestimated her opponents. Mining and Forestry would notice any second now: fish farming, North American southwest shelf, April 2049, *Bingo*.

They'd notice the instant Saturn tampered with the data, too. What to do, what to do?

He could . . . no, the coincidence would be noted too, if he acted now.

He could wait and . . . not good enough.

Retroactively?

If nobody was looking. *Wherever* nobody was looking. *Before* the flags were set in place, four days ago.

To think was to act:

Ten days ago, an exposé on failures in teleoperated

equipment was on record as suppressed by Saturn himself.

A novel about the battle between Agricorp and Mining and Forestry was ready for publication, as listed in the Pocket Books prospectus of *last week*. Saturn sequestered printing presses, trucks, bookstore space. Outlining, quotes, facts were the work of minutes. Writing it would take longer, but such a book needed his conscious attention. Otherwise the prose would come out flat.

A joke during the *Tonight* show monologue, not caught in time, *last night*. Edit those tapes. The reference had reached only the Eastern time zone, North America, and that was why it hadn't been flagged.

Memo to Mining and Forestry, direct from Saturn. They weren't used to that. It would shake them. "You fucked up, citizens. Remember that minor quarrel in which minor people died? Everybody wants to know more about it. Why don't you forget the Shomer girl and try to figure out what went wrong? An Olympic contender's likely to be too busy to write her memoirs, at least for a bit." Leave out mention of the book; "discover" it later. The book was half written; the style needed improving; fiddle with the program . . .

* * *

Nine days after the operation, Jillian began the first fledgling efforts to exercise, to reestablish contact with her body.

She was made of spun glass, cobwebs, and rusty iron filaments, infinitely fragile.

Suryanamaskar, hatha yoga's Sun Salutation, is a series of ten movements linked together with precise breathing. It, and the ancient Chinese movements of T'ai Chi Ch'uan are probably the exercises most expedient for recovery from debilitating illness.

Under Abner's precise direction, she learned it: inhale, reaching high. Exhale, extending the trunk forward and down. Inhale. Exhale as the legs go back in push-up position. Inhale as she straightened her arms into a Cobralike position called Upward Facing Dog. Exhale and lift the hips high, making a pyramid of your body. Inhale as the feet come forward next to the hands. Exhale. Inhale as you return to standing position.

Abner corrected her minutely at every bend and breath. His thin hands changed her posture, spinal alignment, depth of breath, checked her degree of muscle tone. And when he was satisfied, he made her do another one.

She forced it. Sweat exploded from her brow and drooled into her eyes.

The next day, she managed four repetitions. And the next, seven . . .

Within five more days, her energy level approached normal, and most of her flexibility had returned. And there was something else: her balance had improved noticeably. And concentration. And that peculiar effect known as time dilation.

She remembered Osa: the stocky Swede's coordination had been off just a tick. Jillian had to find an exercise that would keep her speed synchronized with her body, so that coordination didn't suffer.

BORIS ©90

Physical effort, physical pain, and bouts of total exhaustion became her life. Anything to keep her mind off the labyrinth of lies that the Council and their world had suddenly become for her. There were answers, but she couldn't get them—not right now.

Even if the Olympiad hadn't demanded her complete attention, Donny, her one certain lead, was unavailable. (According to a vidcast, he was in Jakarta, dedicating a bridge. His smile was a constellation.)

To use Holly's computer again would risk her friend's life. As driven as Jillian was, she couldn't bring herself to do that.

And what was left was study, and planning, and training.

At midnight, thirteen days after the operation, Jillian let herself into the main gymnasium and used her personal ID card to access the Grappler Twelve.

Her body felt completely oiled and powerful, as if she had never violated its envelope of protection. The Grappler waited for her on the mat, a cone of light surrounding it. Its tripod balance arm seemed a saurian tail to her, as if it were a small and friendly dinosaur.

"Program?" the computer requested politely.

"Coordination. Increase speed until ten percent error level, then decrease thirty percent, and replay cycle."

"Program accepted."

She and the Grappler began to dance. It was a formal, noncompetitive exercise, the Grappler's mechanical legs expanding and contracting, its balance shifting every moment as it sought to upend her, to sweep her feet from beneath her, to fling her to the mat.

But at every touch of its padded legs she moved lightly away, delighting in the smoothness and assurance of her own movement. She and the robot flowed together, striving flesh and egoless steel, gleaming with sweat and oil in the single overhead light, for long minutes. The minutes stretched to an hour before Jillian's strength suddenly left her.

She collapsed onto hands and knees, panting, grinning. She watched the sweat drizzle from her face, puddling onto the mat before her. A well of spontaneous, crazed laughter boiled up. She fell over onto her side, whooping.

Then she heard other laughter join hers, followed by the sound of applause. Abner strode out of the shadows. In that moment he didn't seem sick at all, just thin. If he walked like an old man, it was a strong old man, a patriarch, proud and renewed as a man watching the first steps of his grandchild. His eyes were fever-bright.

He beamed down at her. ''You understand,'' he said. ''By God. Osa could never let anyone beat her, let alone a machine. She couldn't do what you just did, Jillian.'' His eyes glowed with admiration.

He stretched out a bony hand to her, and she took it, and drew him down until he was kneeling.

''How much time do you have, Abner?''

Pause. Grim acceptance muted the joy in his face. ''A few months. Maybe. The drugs aren't working as well anymore. But I'll make it to—''

''No.'' She hushed him with her finger. ''Abner.

We've both given up everything. We're both so alone. You've been there for me, and there's nothing I have to give you, no way I have to show you what it's meant. So I'll just ask you. Don't be my coach for a little while, okay? Don't be my teacher.''

"What then?" Their faces were very close.

"My friend," she said. "God, I need a friend."

Abner put his arms around her. She burrowed her face into the notch between cheek and shoulder, and they stayed that way for a time.

Ultimately the gentleness turned into something else, something fiercer and more joyous, with the Grappler as solitary witness.

The Grappler had no ears to hear, or mouth to offer judgment as two lonely human beings found, for a short time at least, a haven from the storm.

But it did have eyes . . .

*　　*　　*

Saturn had seen sex in all its many forms, many times. Over the decades embarrassment had given way to titillation, to amusement, and finally to boredom.

But this one . . . Jillian Shomer interested him. By an athlete's esthetics, her body was perfect. She was coupling with a wasted skeleton of a man. Within a week or so, the sexual function might well have been beyond Abner Collifax completely. One might safely rule out animal lust.

The mating urge? Would she consider him to be good genetic material? He had lost at both the ninth and tenth Olympiads. Surely Jillian Shomer could do better than that.

Pity? Respect? Love perhaps?

Or nothing so noble: the urge to bond an ally? Could Abner be of use to her? Had he information? Skills? Connections that she could access no other way?

Here was meat for the mind. The oddities of human behavior still engaged a jaded intellect after almost a hundred and fifty years.

Another sobering possibility presented itself. Perhaps he was approaching the problem with the wrong tool. Could he have become so used to analytical dissection to resolve problems that he had lost contact with that part of him that felt? Could a being who had lost desire for sexual contact understand the urge? For that matter, could the urge, and all of its manifestations, be understood if approached from a purely mechanistic Newtonian basis? Was *understanding* even possible, in any absolute sense?

His mental smile was a child's, alight with the simple joy of self-discovery.

The Shomer woman was . . . intriguing.

Jillian faced Osa across the mat.

She ignored the glare of the lights and the thirty pairs of eyes watching them. Her whole world was the stocky blond dynamo before her. They circled each other lightly, joined implacably in a combative minuet, wary and nervous as hungry cats.

Confidence and a barely leashed anger boiled within her. Discipline kept a lid on it: the confidence was misplaced. She hadn't been Boosted long enough, hadn't gained enough strength. On the other hand, she would put her timing against anyone in the world.

She had a hole card: Osa held her in contempt. *Never Underestimate Your Enemy.* Combat's deadliest sin. Jillian could surprise the Swedish girl, get to her and take advantage of that contempt and uncertainty before the stronger woman had an opportunity to adjust.

A sudden shift of balance, a hula-movement with hips feinting one way, and shoulders the other. A moment of carefully judged clumsiness, swiftly compensated.

Oh, Osa. I Boosted too late. I'm angry and desperate. Come. Take me.

To a mathematician, judo is a matter of balance points and coefficients of friction, equations of mass and momentum and inertia.

Imagine a cone which must roll onto its edge in order to move, exchanging stability for mobility. It is this movement, in the service of aggression or defense, advance or retreat, that creates vulnerability.

Osa swooped to the attack. Her hands, seeking grips on Jillian's *gi*, were as light as butterflies. Deceptively, hypnotically gentle. Jillian didn't let them deceive her. Once they gained purchase, once Osa found the flaw in her balance, the butterflies would become rocs, talons which lifted and twisted and thundered Jillian down to the mat.

Jillian played fear, played passivity, retreat. She let her breathing catch raggedly, as if fatigued by apprehension. Three times in a minute, Jillian flinched into abortive attacks, barely countering Osa's aggressive defense in time.

Osa's lips pressed together in a pale line, the edges beginning to twitch upward as she gained confidence.

Jillian inhaled, relaxing—

Then in the middle of the breath, exhaled explosively, attacking with a Feral intensity that no human being could have anticipated or countered.

With timing perfect to the millisecond, Jillian swept Osa's ankle at the instant when weight transferred from one leg to the other. It was as if the Swedish girl had trod on the proverbial banana peel. They crashed to the mat together, Jillian in control.

The rest happened in a single cycle of breath:

Moving in the eerie slow-motion world created by total focus, she trapped Osa's forearm in her right armpit, swung her legs up in a body scissors. As they hit the mat she adjusted the scissors so that her ankles pinioned Osa's throat.

Osa heaved once, titanically, twisted like a beached eel, tensed her throat and arm and drummed her heels on the mat seeking balance that Jillian refused to let her find.

Another spasm—but Jillian only bore down more viciously.

And then—

She slapped Jillian's leg, choosing submission over unconsciousness or injury.

Osa coughed, then rolled away as Jillian released her, face dark with anger.

Jillian heaved for air, speckles of light dancing in her eyes, muscles shaking with the sudden intensity of the effort.

For ten seconds the two women stared at each other, motionless, twin ivory images carved with flame.

Then, slowly, Osa regained composure and forced herself to smile.

She stood as Jillian stood. Osa flicked imaginary dust from her *gi*, still eyeing her opponent with new respect.

Then slowly, and with immense solemnity, she bowed.

The vacuum tube car was wall-to-wall Olympians, their coaches and luggage. They traveled at just under orbital speed, deep underground. There were no windows, but then again there was nothing to see.

In the forward car a classic flatfilm played, electronically modified so that one Olympian after another replaced Humphrey Bogart or Katherine Hepburn aboard the *African Queen*. When they tired of that, they replaced the two stars with other performers. After trying a half-dozen current male matinee idols, including a gibbon who performed in Aslan, they settled on a fortyish Sean Connery. To fill Hepburn's spinster role, they recruited the image of an Australian beauty queen named Brigitte Chan-Smythe. Chan-Smythe had recently scandalized Transportation with pornographic satires of their most recent advertising campaign. Dialogue and action were enthusiastically improvised.

Conversations ran sluggishly in the aft car. Maybe the occupants felt the close quarters, or the gigatons of earth and sea above, or the pull of vacuum and the dark.

But in the middle car they eschewed passive entertainment, retracted the seats and danced. At a quarter gravity all dances were slow, to music three centuries old. Eldren Cowan taught English Regency line dancing to tapes he had brought for his Spirit Event.

Jillian curtsied to Jeff Tompkins, solemnly linked arms with him, and revolved carefully. Too much enthusiasm in low gravity could send an Olympian caroming into a wall, to the vast amusement of all but Eldren.

Gravity returned: the track led up, the cars began to slow. Jillian excused herself and made her way to the movie car.

Connery and Chan-Smythe had just sunk the German warship, and were celebrating in a manner probably envisioned, but certainly never filmed, by John Huston. With a final roar of appreciation the film was terminated, and someone conjured up a map of the subway.

Jillian just glimpsed the world-girdling network as the scale began to zero in on the deep Atlantic tunnel . . . on the Aegean Sea . . . on Greece . . . It was like watching a computer program take the Mandelbrot Set to finer and finer scale. Major subway trunks ran across continents, coast to coast, under mountains and deserts and farmland. Bigger channels yet ran beneath the oceans. The view ran up from beneath the Atlantic, took a branch that ran beneath the Aegean, out of the sea to Greece, chose from hundreds of branches . . . the view zeroed in on Athens, on ghostly city streets, following the moving dot that was themselves.

Funny, she'd never noticed that the world's subway system was designed as fractals.

The cars turned smoothly; they twitched as other cars matched or detached. Presently the doors opened on light and sound.

Athens Convention Center. Hundreds of anonymous human shapes milled near the terminals, held back by ropes and security forces as they waved placards and chanted welcome. Jillian returned to her seat.

There on the narrow cushions Abner stirred restlessly from his nap. He slept a great deal lately, husbanding his energy, perhaps, or seeking in unconsciousness a muting of the ceaseless pain.

His eyes opened, took a few seconds to focus. His face was more brutally weathered by the Boost now, and his breathing was more labored. Sometimes she listened to it at night as he slept. She dreaded its irregularity, imagined that she heard in it a cry for peace, a weariness of body that extended, finally, even to the spirit which animated the withered shell.

"We're here," he said. His lips lifted at the corners. "I promised myself I'd make it this far."

"We're not done here yet, Abner." She gripped his hand as if by strength alone she could halt his deterioration. "You can't leave me until I've won."

The subway eased through a seal, and air hissed into the lock. The Olympians hooted, hustled up out of their seats, and began to unload their gear.

She waited. Abner shouldn't even have been on a general passenger train. He could be hurt in the press.

The aisle began to empty toward the front, and she stood, snaked out past Abner, and helped him to his feet.

Like a granddaughter helping a beloved but doddering elder to cross the street, Jillian escorted Abner, took both of their bags in tow, helped him out into the terminal.

A Greek band oompah'd its way through a bizarre medley of ''God Bless America'' and Transportation's corporate anthem, ''Songs from the Sky.'' A few Olympians automatically stiffened to attention. Jillian scanned the Olympians until she saw Holly. The biologist was fighting hard to swallow a sardonic grin.

As they flowed toward the line of waiting shuttles they were showered by confetti and streamers, cheered, given all of the fanfare that Jillian had craved on departure from Boston. Now it was too late. Now she didn't really give a damn.

Rain swept down in curtains, wavering across the pavement like bed sheets blowing on a clothesline. The crowd eddied like ocean waves, frantic to see the arriving athletes. She could not see faces. Their faces were darkened, backlit ovals.

A pool of light: they were close enough now for her to make out a sign printed in Greek, Japanese, and English. The English read: STOP THE OLYMPICS. The protester was clearly visible for a moment, face no lon-

ger an indistinguishable smear, now a twisting, screaming mouth and a fringe of sopping hair. Then security men moved swiftly from the sides, and he vanished into the shadows.

Some of the others strutted and posed for the crowds, flexing muscles, smiling broadly. Holly held up a briefcase containing her precious files, waving confidently to the cameras.

Holly was ready. Her studies on the immune system were complete and broken down into display mode. If they didn't win her the gold, they might still save her from the effects of Boost.

Maybe. The world would change.

"Quite a show, isn't it?" Abner said as their car glided away through the crowd.

The press of humanity actually thickened for the first hundred feet or so, then thinned out. Then they were on the road and heading out of the terminal.

Jillian felt like hiding. "Why do I get the feeling that I haven't seen anything yet?"

"Because you are a bright, perceptive girl."

*　　*　　*

The caravan to Olympic Bay took half an hour.

The floating islands were tethered in standard three-by-three resort formation. Each hosted a network of dormitories, gymnasiums, cafeterias, and entertainment facilities. They were fortified and fenced, protected on all sides: a temporary luxury community created to fill every Olympian need.

Olympic Bay glittered in the misty rain like a

mythical mountain fortress, and Jillian felt her pulse race.

Ferry skimmers were coasting in on plumes of steaming foam. Helicopters and floatcars braved the wind to reach landing pads. And from every vehicle streamed Olympians and their coaches.

Jillian helped Abner onto the docking platform, hustled him to a two-passenger robot monotram. It surged forward the moment they were seated.

Abner's thin fingers tapped against the glass, and he sighed audibly.

"What is it?" Jillian asked as they drew up to one of the condos. It rose up out of an artificial hillside on enormous aluminum stilts. An escalator rippled up the side of the hill to the main entrance. Rain was deflected by a silver awning.

"All the rest of it was just rehearsal, Jill. I can't help you anymore."

Was he asking permission to die? Abner seemed translucent, ephemeral.

"It may be I don't need you," she said in a voice she might have used with a child. "But I want you to see me win."

His hands slid down into his lap, were still. "All right."

She kissed his cheek as the tram stopped and the door slid open. "I'll be in touch."

"Please."

A silver-garbed young man offered to carry Jillian's luggage for her, and she declined. She shrugged the strap over her shoulder and straightened up, stepping onto the escalator.

The little monotram disappeared around a curve.

Holly waited for her at the top of the escalator. "Where's Abner going?"

"A Medtech Intensive. He's going to need life-support soon." The wind whipped a spray of rain into her face. With the tip of her tongue she tasted it. Salt. "Real soon."

"Is he septic?"

She shrugged. "It's a miracle he's hung on this long. He'll make it another month. Bet on it."

They stood and watched the crowd gather and thin on the dock, ebbing and surging as a tide. Holly chuckled, calculatedly changing the mood. "I've never seen so much healthy flesh in all my life. I wonder if the rumors are true."

Curiosity nudged Jillian out of her pensive mood. "What rumors?"

"Ah, you know." Holly leaned over, stage-whispered conspiratorially. "They say that the most intense sex in the known universe takes place in the Olympic villages."

"I've heard that. Are you planning a little personal inquiry?"

"Certainly. A series of controlled experiments in the name of science."

"Double-blind, I suppose."

"I'll keep one eye open."

*   *   *

A pair of gorgeous young male attendants escorted them to their separate rooms. Jillian's, a tall, darkly Mediterranean lad who looked usefully fit, offered to help Jillian unpack. He also offered to rub her feet, massage her lower back, or perform any other service that might be required. He was cute, but she declined.

When the door closed, she began to unpack. She placed shoes beneath her bed, tested the bed, hung pantsuits and dresses in the closet, squirreled toiletries away in the bathroom. She busied herself around and around the room, unaware that she was being watched until Holly cleared her throat from the doorway.

"You know," the biologist said thoughtfully, "you are definitely not the same anxious little girl I met eight weeks ago."

Jillian sat on the bed, unnaturally aware of the play of every muscle as it flexed and knotted. She felt like a bundle of live wires. "What's the difference?"

"You . . ." Holly closed her eyes, stared into the darkness for a few seconds before answering. "Your eyes don't have any humor in them, but your mouth is smiling all the time. There's just something a little distant about you. Detached."

Jillian's lips curled up, but there was no warmth in them. "Well, maybe I finally got the joke, Holly."

Suddenly, Holly seemed very uncomfortable, found it difficult to meet Jillian's gaze. "Uh-huh," she said. "Well. Maybe so."

Holly seemed in a hurry to leave, and Jillian did nothing to stop her.

Jillian stared down at her hands, felt the play of tendon and muscle in her forearms, closed her eyes to hear the slow thunder of her heartbeat.

The Boost was speeding up. She could feel the changes, feel her body growing and shifting. She wiggled her toes and could mentally isolate every tendon, muscle, and nerve fiber. Every breath reverberated hollowly in the cavern of her chest.

Where was Jillian Shomer? Here, on the edge of a bed in a strange room, in a strange place a world away from her beginnings?

And if not . . . then who was she?

She had wanted Abner to come with her, and was ashamed of the true reason. They spoke of companionship, of support, of coaching, directly of affection and obliquely of love. The truth was darker.

Abner was rotting inside. Impending death enshrouded him like a fetid cloak. Death was in his eyes, his movement, his precarious balance. It creaked in his voice.

Jillian Shomer, more vital than ever before, was morbidly fascinated. Abner was a living reminder of the hell which awaited her if she failed.

She felt as if she were falling through a black hole toward some ultimate encounter with a Jillian that had never been.

Jillian looked up at the wall clock, and jumped. Two hours had passed, time during which she sat motionless, listened to her body grow and change, felt the heat as her blood raced to remove toxins and rebuild tissue.

She shucked herself out of her clothes, lay back, told the ceiling light to shut down.

There were ways to deal with jet lag. Tension, too. Boost made it even easier.

She writhed in the dark, stretching and tensing each muscle in individual sequence. Back, side, belly . . .

. . . rolled out of bed, dressed, moved into the silent hallways. From far away, another floor perhaps, came sounds of merriment. She saw no one in the halls.

Outside the rain had stilled, leaving the silver trail of the escalator glistening with its memory. She took the escalator down two levels, and caught a submarine tram to the shore.

The little tube cars were nine parts entertainment excursion and one part practical transportation. Fish slipped in and out of the floodlamps. Jillian stared up through the transparent tram walls as they hissed along. The water turned black just a few yards beyond the lamps. Fish flashed to life, then vanished utterly. There might have been nothing below her or above her, or anything at all in the universe except this tiny capsule cruising through an endless sea.

A young woman in a silver blazer with an Olympic patch greeted her at a shoreside tram station. In heavily accented English she asked if Jillian would require a limousine, or an escort. Jillian demurred, and mounted the upward escalator alone.

What the night required was a walk. The mists of evening were cleansing, comforting. The stadia were less than a mile from the dock.

Electricians and cameramen, carpenters and painters were still busy, working like a colony of well-disciplined termites to prepare the stadia and surrounding environs. The main stadium rose like the

Coliseum of old, a structure a quarter mile long and fifteen stories high, with seats for a hundred thousand spectators.

Just as Olympians had been arriving half the night, so had their audience. From all over the world they came, flooding the hotels in Athens, overflowing out to smaller artificial islands in the bay. Live spectator seating in three different arenas, holo feeds winging out to the world and beyond, the Olympiad would be watched by three billion people. Those who stayed home would have a better view.

They were a legion of three thousand, the new gladiators, joined in mortal combat with something infinitely more terrible than lions.

Jillian stood in the shadows, watching: someone else had had the inspiration for a late-night stroll.

A slender man in a silver windbreaker was running laps on the track. He was singing as he ran. His voice was beautifully cultured, and barely seemed affected by the rigors of a pace that accelerated to something near sprinting. As he circled the track and came closer she could make out the words he sang:

He's never, ever sick at sea!
What, never?
No, never . . .
Well, hardly ever . . .

As he passed her she saw the Bulgarian flag on the back of his jacket, beneath Agricorp's crossed stalks of wheat. She recognized him from a *Newsweek* loop on the transport in from Denver.

He slowed to a jog and ran out of the stadium, trailing song behind.

Jillian walked out to the middle of the field, sat cross-legged in the wet grass. Uncounted tons of concrete, tens of thousands of foam-steel girders, millions of man-hours had gone into building this stadium.

Here, track-and-field events would take place.

A roofed oval to the north was reserved for swimming and gymnastics, weight lifting and judo, fencing and archery and the other indoor events.

A third location, also domed, would house the academic and esthetic events. Chess, flight simulation, computer art, oral interpretation, all of the skills that would mean success for some and disaster for others.

In these three stadia, and in a selected location in the mountains to the north, Jillian would display her gifts and talents. Here she would stretch her body and mind and heart to the maximum. She prayed that it would be enough.

She noticed something. For the first time in her life, as she prayed, there was no sense of praying to something outside herself. Her prayer was directed to a new Jillian, the creature growing inside a chrysalis composed of the old Jillian's hair and eyes and hopes and fears. Splitting away now. Another creature. Stronger. Fiercer.

It heard her prayer, and hissed its savage reply.

*   *   *

The noon sun gleamed down on them. Row after glittering row they came, the Olympians. They carried, according to their allegiances, corporate or national banners. Three thousand strong, every human color, from every corner of the planet they came.

Jillian stood shoulder to shoulder with strangers. She stole a glance back through the pack. Holly was back there, somewhere. They couldn't stand together: Holly owed allegiance to Medtech, as Osa did to Agricorp.

She peered around, caught sight of Mary Ling, the tiny Taiwanese girl said to be one of the toughest competitors in the fell-running division.

But Ling wasn't as formidable as Catherine St. Clair, the English Medtech chemist who was not only a top fell-runner, but had worked on the five-man British Academy of Science team which garnered last year's Nobel Prize in medicine. St. Clair was a strong chess player and a stunning redhead to boot. Jillian gritted her teeth.

So they marched in their pockets and rows, carrying their banners and singing their songs, saluting the crowd that overflowed the stands and spread out across the world. They were best of the best, three thousand of the finest minds and bodies that had ever strode the planet.

Within seven years, ninety-eight percent of them would be dead. There were just fifty open slots among the Linked.

As the anthems of two dozen nations and sixteen corporations played, they marched. Speeches were made. Fireworks were ignited, and a gigantic One-World hologram, the Council's ultimate emblem, rotated overhead.

From the north corner of the stadium, a lone figure ran with the grace of a gazelle, carrying on high a torch which smoked and flickered in the still air.

The stadium fell into a hush, and every eye watched as a thin, pale man entered the stands and sprinted up a carpeted stair to touch the flame to the official Olympic torch.

The crowd relaxed into a collective sigh, and then exploded into applause.

The Olympics had begun.

In the Arts and Entertainments auditorium eighteen thousand people sat in their patient rows.

Jillian Shomer scanned their faces, striving to read their minds, their hearts. If each of them were deep-scanned, so that she could read their heart rates and blood pressures, skin temperatures and EEGs . . . would it help her to talk to them?

The question, the doubt, the yearning to touch the faceless audience, had plagued artists since the beginning of time. Technology had changed nothing.

"Ladies and gentlemen, Miss Jillian Shomer. Division: Spirit. Presentation: Fractal Art."

Picture: glaciers, advancing from different directions, meeting in a central fissure in the earth, grinding the countryside into gravel and splinters.

As the holographic images materialized in the dome of the main theater, Jillian distanced herself from reality, allowed herself to pretend that she had not created these images through countless hours of programming. She became instead a spectator, a student attending a phantasmal geology lecture.

The ice was spectacularly varicolored. Where two moving cliff faces struck one another, clouds of steam boiled forth. The image expanded swiftly. The camera POV glided into the steam; the curls and wisps and patterns of light became clear. The images revealed were not confined to curlicues and arcs: networks of edge and angle emerged. As they pushed deeper into the scene, the image paradoxically reverted to the macro image.

Here again was the ocean of crawling ice . . . but a hole seemed to have been torn in the bottom of the world. The floes crunched and swirled in a slow-motion whirlpool. The grinding scream of a million million tons of ice filled the auditorium. Darkness congealed into a dense strip of jumbled cubes and triangles that pulsed with the roar like an optical sound track.

The sound itself was a repeating pattern.

Geometric pulses shone so bright, loomed so large that they stunned the senses. Chunks of angle broke free, coalesced into glaciers once again. The glaciers crashed, gouged mountains from their path, and tore simplified redwoods up by their roots.

The image expanded once again, pushed into the trees themselves. The pattern of the leaves was a repeating pattern, its angles and cool green geometries fading to outline to produce crystals, ice crystals which were once again glaciers.

And again two walls of ice met screaming. The computer simulation expanded the scene, took the judges and audience to some new aspect of that primal scape. With color, depth, shape, sound, and movement Jillian conjured up the infinite variations of pattern within pattern, until the repetitions became a musical movement, the entire ebb and flow of change the heartbeat of an enormous creature from ages past, the living fire of its breath a dance of creation and destruction.

She'd found the core of this while exploring something nearly outside her field: the torpid formation and flow of plasma between the core and rim of a spiral galaxy: the laws that govern a transgalactic lightning bolt. Her very simple equation might not describe such a process in all detail, but as the basis for a visual display . . . In Jillian's humble opinion, it made the Mandelbrot Set look like a six-year-old's first attempt at needlepoint.

*   *   *

The sequence ended. The lights came up full.

Nervous at the lack of response, Jillian stood, looking out at the thousands of spectators, perhaps twelve thousand who had come to witness her presentation.

Finally, someone near the judges' box began to applaud, and the clapping became infectious, until the entire auditorium rocked with applause.

Overwhelmed, Jillian took her bow, keeping her eyes on the scoreboards as the officials rendered their judgment.

9.1
9.2
8.7

A respectable score. Saturn thought that the Shomer woman could take a silver with that.

Interesting mind.

She was capable, and creative, and intelligent enough. And . . . unpredictable. Driven by motivations he didn't quite understand. She bore further examination.

As did her associate Holly Lakein.

Saturn scanned all of the inputs from the Olympiad, as he did inputs from around the Earth and to the outer reaches of the solar system.

Lakein's performance on the balance beam had been stunning, a gold. Her modern dance display was less impressive—all force and altitude, technique masquerading as emotion.

But her chess . . . ah.

A mind that can think thousands of moves ahead can take no pleasure in the winning or losing of such a game. But there was beauty in the patterns of her play.

Her five matches tested her to the limit. Her second opponent was Catherine St. Clair. Saturn recognized motifs developed by Botvinnik in the Netherlands, Alekhine in Zurich, Korchnoi in Leningrad.

Lakein was experimental, bold, and innovative. St.

Clair played a straightforward pressure game, grinding attrition which could well have crippled a lesser player. Ultimately St. Clair had taken a pawn sacrifice which developed into a forked check. Five moves later she retired, congratulating an exhausted Holly on a brilliant coup.

It was Holly Lakein's finest moment. Overall, she bronzed, and Saturn knew that she had only one more hope: her molecular biology presentation.

Saturn effortlessly broke through Lakein's security codes, decrypted her files, and scanned her paper on alternative avenues for Boost control.

Again, impressive. She presented her case clearly and creatively, and had obviously had access to classified data. She quoted none of it, but some of her conclusions would have been impossible, her lines of reasoning corrupted, unless she had seen . . . perhaps the 2046 RAND study.

But she could not hope for gold, and without gold, Holly could not possibly Link.

Too bad. Still, she had another four years. Then there were Saturn's own priorities . . .

Again he turned attention to the Arts and Entertainments auditorium, now emptying. One of the judges was a guest Counselor, Aziltov from Communications, who had given Jillian a 9.2. He seemed still fascinated by the empty stage. No doubt he was replaying the fractal art display in his mind, with the exactitude possible only to a Linked.

And then he would probably do it again. And again. Aziltov had developed an unhealthy tendency to replay pleasurable moments. Or invent them.

Aziltov was borderline Feral.

The world was a fracturing dike to Saturn, and he was a little Dutch boy with a thousand busy wet fingers.

*   *   *

Abner was conscious, but barely so. The machines breathed for him, filtered his blood, kept the pain at bay.

Some pain remained. He dared not slip too deeply into narcosis. Blocking the nerves electrically left him in a disassociated state that unraveled sanity even more swiftly.

He desperately wanted to see Jillian compete.

She visited him daily, speaking to him of strategy, or trivial things, and he wondered if she knew how he had lied to her.

A white lie, certainly. He'd made a mistake, mentioning the illiteracy paper. No Russian had written it. Her precious Donny had won gold with the damned thing.

The paper had won gold, and then been buried, damn them all to hell.

On the holoscreen, Jillian approached the mat, bowed to her second opponent.

She closed, and the Boost-accelerated reflexes of both opponents made the action a blur. Ordinarily he would have slowed the images down, inspected them frame by frame. But he was so tired, and hurt so badly. Only one more thing now, and he could let go.

His attention had wandered. Jillian was in a pretzel with her opponent, a straining tangle of arms and legs. The other girl's shoulders were pinned to the mat.

Jillian stood, victorious.

Abner closed his eyes, smiling, as the screen went dark. The nurses had programmed it to turn on only when Jillian was competing, to allow him to save his strength. Abner slipped away into an uneasy sleep, a dim dream world, its horizon boiling black with locusts.

A buzzing filled the room. He opened his eyes, managed to rub some of the gum out of them.

Jillian. Osa. Competing for gold.

"Oh, Jillian. Darn it all to heck." He mentally repeated that last sentence, and gloomily decided that Jillian was a bad influence.

He had hoped that the Scandinavian would have fouled out, or been beaten, or broken an arm. Anything to keep her away from Jillian.

They went at each other like a pair of dervishes. Long phrases of careful circling, light touches, and then a blinding flurry of movement. Osa took her opponent dead seriously this time, used her phenomenal agility to keep Jillian from closing.

Then . . . an opening. Jillian took Osa to the mat, slamming her down so brutally hard that Abner winced and grinned at the same time.

Jillian went for the pin . . . was straining for the hold . . .

And went limp. Abner cursed. Osa had shammed, let Jillian try to pin, and had worked herself into a choking position.

The screen went black.

Fell-running was still a hope, but he was so tired.

And the pain. He just couldn't take the pain much longer. He would have to ask for drugs, and Blocking. And then he would slide down that final hole, and couldn't be sure of ever coming up again.

There was still something to say to Jillian, but he could no longer be sure of his ability to say it.

*　　*　　*

Jillian had two chances at the athletic events. The judo which had so tested her body and spirit had yielded a respectable silver. The fractal art presentation had yielded silver, but her thesis on chaos theory and sociology had only earned a bronze. Not good enough. The fell-running had become do-or-die.

Traditionally, fell-running is a European sport. Not until the third Olympiad had it become a truly international pastime. Competitors traverse a ten-kilometer obstacle course, facing natural and artificial barriers.

There should have been eleven women on line with Jillian. Nine were there. Two were Boosted veterans who had no chance of linking, who had been quietly removed from the Olympiad in the name of security.

Four of the women, including St. Clair, were of purely European extraction. Three held varying degrees of African blood in their veins. One was the sinewy Taiwanese, Mary Ling.

Jillian settled down into a comfortable crouch, heel against the block, and waited.

The changes within her body had peaked—she hoped. She felt all whipcord and whalebone, every nerve fiber aflame. She glared at the other women on the line, and their eyes held no warmer welcome.

She wouldn't just beat them. She would crush them.

The gun sounded. Jillian exploded out of the blocks.

Fell-running is conducted over savage, broken terrain: rocks, boulders, ravines. There was no clearly marked path, and it was up to each participant to make her way through the course to a predetermined finish line in a minimum of time.

She could go around, stay to level ground, and add miles to her run. She could go directly over, using pitons, or she could ''cut the edges,'' free climbing, trusting her agility and strength to deal with the obstacles as they came.

Jillian paused, consulting her compass. She was heading northwest. It was eleven in the morning, and the sun would begin its descent soon. She fixed its arc in her mind, swore to herself that she wouldn't consult the compass again, and began to climb.

Thirty yards to her left, Mary Ling was ascending a pile of boulders with the confidence of a spider monkey.

Jillian herself had screwed her concentration down to a narrow beam. ''Black dot'' focus, she called it. She was aware of the rest of the world, even if concentrating on the next rock, the next step, the next moment.

''White dot'' focus would build an attention so extreme that the rest of the world seemed to disappear. Fine for playing chess. Dangerous for a fell-runner.

She had reached the top of a cairn of rock, pulling herself up into shadow, breathing deeply and evenly. One more toehold would bring her to safety.

She sensed more than saw the rock as it fell. Jillian released her left hand's grip, swung out to the right as the rock whistled past.

Her reflexive swing back to the left took her into the path of a second rock. It glanced off the cliff face next to her arm, and struck her shoulder.

Jillian's left side went numb. She skidded, lost her purchase and found it again. Gasping, she stared down the column of rock. If she had fallen, it would have meant a fractured leg, at the least.

And hadn't there been a flicker of a human shadow up above her? And hadn't she heard something very like retreating footsteps?

She hung there, distant from the pain in her shoulder, gasping. She began to climb again, more slowly now. Her mind burned with anger, and that anger pushed aside all fatigue, all fear, leaving only the climb.

She reached the level, and glanced around swiftly, crouching. Nothing. A floatcar whirred up behind her, its camera doubtless recording her intrepid efforts.

She ran now, picking her way through the rocks as quickly as she could. The anger seethed in her, fueled by suspicion, and the urge to find her tormenter.

Exhaustion clawed at her. She ignored it, buried it under a layer of discipline so deep that she would die rather than yield.

The sun beat down on her, glaring off the rocks as she crossed the mesa, and she stole another glimpse at her compass, making a slight correction.

She had cut as much distance as she dared from her time. Now it was—

A scream. It was short, and despairing, and

abruptly cut off by the dull, heavy sound of a human body impacting a shelf of rock.

Jillian put on a burst of speed. The sound had come from in front of her. Someone ahead of her had—

At the edge of the mesa was a decline, steeper than the ascent but with better hand and foot holds. And a hundred feet below her, a rag doll crushed by an angry child, was Catherine St. Clair.

Halfway down the face was Mary Ling. The Taiwanese paused, glared up at Jillian, face tight with challenge.

Or concentration.

It *could* have been an accident.

Jillian's own concentration was shot now. As she climbed down the cliff she had to pass within five feet of the woman's body. She tried to confine her thoughts to her breathing, to the smooth flow of muscles in shoulders and hips. But then St. Clair, shattered on the rocks, suddenly moved. Her body arched, and her mouth made a wet keening sound.

From somewhere behind her came the burring whistle of a Medtech aircar coming in for a pickup. It was still seconds away. Catherine St. Clair tried to move, tried to turn. Her eyes stared at Jillian without focusing. Jillian was frozen to the rock face, unmoving, until the woman from Kenya descended past her.

She snapped out of her trance then, and started to move, but the Englishwoman stretched out her hand and tried to say something like "Help me . . ." except that the words came out as an indecipherable groan, all vowels and wet consonants.

Where was the Medtech vehicle? She couldn't leave.

St. Clair's eyes locked with hers, and Jillian saw her die, saw the lights go out, the body collapse into lifelessness.

Shaking now, Jillian completed her descent.

Her control was shattered. She was already breathing hard, her ankle felt swollen, and her shoulder had little strength.

It was a straight run now to the finish line, and she was in third place, with Mary Ling twenty feet ahead of her.

Jillian bore down, willed her legs to pump faster and faster, ignored the pain. Ignored everything but that final sprint to the finish line, to the reward that awaited her if she could only overcome the fatigue built up over the week of competition.

Her entire body was aflame now, but she couldn't and wouldn't stop. She had cut the distance between herself and the Taiwanese to perhaps ten feet, still gaining, five feet now, three feet—

Then, from some unimaginable well of hidden resources, Mary Ling seemed to go into another gear, and simply pulled away from her, crossing the finish line a full eight feet ahead of Jillian Shomer.

The shock of it almost drove Jillian off her feet. Her entire body began to shake, as if every strand of connective tissue were suddenly unraveling. She lurched the last few feet, collapsed across the finish line.

She tasted dust, and defeat, and death.

Chapter

13

A mile away, in the central stadium, the crowds were cheering.

Jillian watched as speeches were made. The winners paraded proudly alongside those losers who had, in Donny's fevered phrasing, "the strength of character, the wisdom and depth of commitment to share in the true spirit of the games, to rejoice in the uplifting of the human race without the hunger for personal gain." And she watched him present the gold medal to that little Taiwanese slut.

Abner had been awash in pain medication by the time she got to his room. He mumbled words that might have been comforting if they had been comprehensible. His eyes were closed—she'd thought he'd gone to sleep—when he said clearly: "Check the records. Check my records."

"Records? Abner, *which* records?"

"O . . . lym . . . piad."

He had slipped further and further away from her, into delirium. His words and thoughts became ever more garbled. Jillian sat beside him in a darkening room, feeling her bruises and scrapes, watching Abner Warren Collifax slide into the same pit which would, in five or six years, yawn to welcome her.

For twenty hours she sat there, a statue of flesh, watching him wither before her eyes. With all of her strength she willed him to speak, to breathe, to live.

In vain. After twenty hours he died.

Numb, Jillian tucked the sheet around his neck, kissed his forehead, and left quietly, almost on tiptoe, as if he were merely asleep.

More loss:

Walking back to the dorm along the edge of the island. A warm Mediterranean evening, falling swiftly. A sweet heavy breeze swayed in from the south.

Activity over next to one of the low sea walls. A half-dozen silver blazers, the sudden appearance of a Medtech tram.

Something wet and limp was hauled up from the ocean. Jillian caught a momentary image of flaccid, heavy muscle, dripping water. Vulnerable nakedness. Wet black hair, shadow-dappled by dying sunlight.

An easy death. Anesthetized by the cold, put to sleep by oxygen starvation—What was that, in the shadows off to the right? Broken, shattered: something

in the darkness. Jillian stepped quietly to it, bent, watching her fingers tremble as she reached.

Half of Jeff Tompkins's palace was still perfect, a study in ivory. Half was stove in as if by a sudden, terrible effort, one of those moments of madness which, once done, cannot be undone.

Even partly crushed, the model was exquisite, a monument to his persistence and skill. But it hadn't been good enough. In the end, Jeff's castle had been not of ivory, but of sand.

A silver girl took the model from her hands and waved a wordless Jillian away from the scene.

Back in her room she watched the Olympics closing down. She was too heavy and limp to move. From beyond her window machine noises ebbed and flowed as helicopters, boats, and skimmers arrived to take the losers away.

A nebula of fireworks exploded above the coliseum. Jillian heard their distant thunder, could see the brief bright promise of their flame wavering through a sheen of tears.

For hours she sat there, until the fireworks died and the stadium emptied, and the spectators began their long exodus. The room was illuminated only by yellow-orange streetlights and the distant glow of the Athens cityscape. Intermittently, limos cruised or floatcars drifted past her window, their headlights piercing her shadows.

She flexed her hands in the darkness.

The door swung open, and Holly stood there, hipshot and gently mocking, resplendent in frilly pink chiffon that plunged and gathered and teased, and contrasted beautifully with her dark skin.

She pirouetted, and the dark waters of Jillian's grief grew shallow. "Poetry," Jillian croaked, and managed a smile.

Holly took Jillian in her arms, comforting, and finally Jillian let go in great whooping sobs. Holly stroked the back of her head.

"Do you want me to stay here with you?" Holly whispered. "All you have to do is say the word . . ."

"How do you do it?" Jillian's voice was low and hoarse. "You lost, and you act like you won."

"I've got four years to try again, and I've got insurance," Holly answered, as kindly as she could. "I believe in myself."

"You may be the smartest person here." Jillian sniffed. "You go to that party tonight. Whoop it up for both of us."

"A promise." Holly smiled. "And another one: if I make it, we'll both make it, lady. Remember that."

Jillian started to protest, to say something about honor, and chances taken, and perhaps something trite about dice rolling as they may. Holly hushed her.

"Trust me, Jillian. And listen: you're not Linked, but you've earned more Comnet time. We can help each other, Jillian. We're going to help each other, understand?"

"All right. Now, get out of here, go to the party. Enjoy yourself."

They hugged again, more fiercely this time, and then Holly left.

The city was settling down to sleep, gradually deflating after two weeks of media gluttony. Reflected in the glass was a woman Jillian didn't know, a woman who had abandoned everything familiar, and had no-where left to turn.

For the thousandth time, she inserted the plastic chip into its slot, saw the error message appear, and knew just how big a fool she had been.

Took the card out, tenderly tucking it back into her purse.

It was seven steps to the bathroom. She had mea-sured them. Eventually she would need to know the distance to the medicine cabinet.

There were pain tabs and sleeping tabs in there. Just peel back the protective strip and press the adhe-sive edge onto a pulse point. One was enough to en-sure a sound night's sleep. Ultimately she would increase the dosage until even Abner's deep, devour-ing pain floated away from her, leaving her in soothing oblivion.

She felt the play of webbed muscles in her fore-arms, sensed the strength and inhuman precision of her every motion. Being human hadn't been enough. Today she was stronger, faster, better than she had ever been in her life. It still hadn't been enough. God damn it, it hadn't been enough.

She'd be twenty-seven by the next Olympiad. How could she take a gold in judo? Or even place as highly as she had this time? She was over the hill for competition. She was walking around, dead.

She pushed against the window, felt its slight bend, guessed at its thickness.

There. She felt the exact angle to push. She could rip it right out of its track. Could shatter it. She and the shards of glass could go tumbling down to the

pavement below, down into the night place where
Beverly waited . . .

It would be sin. And she shouldn't have blas-
phemed.

Jillian offered a quick prayer for forgiveness, then
slammed her palm against the glass plate.

There were questions left unanswered.

Abner had left a hint.

She didn't need anything elaborate to access public files. She used the building's computer. What was
it that Abner had said? Check the records?

The 2044 Olympiad?

Nothing classified *there*.

She quickly found herself skimming through four-
year-old images, stopping whenever something interesting occurred. There was the usual scattering of
"Classified" notices. She wished she could have borrowed Holly's Void. From a Void, she might have figured out ways past the security blocks, and any
information she got would be absorbed much faster.
But this would get her there.

She sorted for Abner, and his records came up on
the screen swiftly. His judo wins were famous, and
she had studied them a thousand times. It was still
startling to see him at the peak of his physical prowess,
a wiry streak of quicksilver. He'd made a decent showing in fell-running, a bronze, and in Arts his recital of
original poetry had won an ovation, if not a gold.

His last category had been abstract sociology, sim-
ilar to her own. His paper had explored the emergence
of a pseudomatriarchal leadership structure in the
American prison systems.

She scanned for Pushkin's name . . .

And found it, but *his* paper was on the rebirth of Keynesian economics.

Confused now, she called up the list of competitors and . . .

Donny Crawford's name jumped out at her. The subject of his paper?

Classified.

Donny had taken the gold, of course. Abner had lied. He'd given her a clue, then backed off when he realized she could get in trouble. Donny Crawford excelled at everything he touched. He had taken gold in one athletic event, and two academic categories. One of his papers had been implemented. One hidden.

She doubled back to social theory, and scanned to be sure she had missed nothing. She hadn't. Donny Crawford was the only choice.

Jillian turned off the console, and stood.

Well.

She hadn't wanted to go to the party, but maybe there was something for her to do there after all.

*   *   *

The main ballroom of the Arts and Entertainments pavilion was thinning out. A few couples still swayed to live music, a few conversations still percolated around the refreshment tables.

She attached herself to a group of revelers. They slapped her on the back, got her drinks, called her a hell of a good sport, and were too drunk to look carefully at her eyes, to notice that she wasn't drinking at all.

To see that her eyes rarely strayed far from Donny. He was still there, smiling and nodding and officially congenial. And Mary Ling was standing so close to him, taking every marginally discreet opportunity to rub against him, marking off her territory.

Jillian gritted her teeth, searched the room, and found Holly dancing with a knot of pleasantly inebriated Olympians. All had placed, none had won gold or silver.

They weren't really dancing in partners. They were a group, moving in intense rhythm, tribal rhythm perhaps, trying to lose their emotional pain in a cocktail of endorphins and alcohol.

Holly waved a glassy hello, and went into an even more violent gyration.

Jillian joined them, keeping one eye on Donny and his vixen. She couldn't really forget herself, couldn't really lose the pain, but it helped, made the ache of waiting more endurable.

Holly handed her a glass of spiked punch. Jillian hesitated, and then gulped it down greedily. Then another.

Minutes passed, and songs changed. By the time Donny and Mary made their excuses and headed for the door, the room was spinning pleasantly.

Jillian waited five minutes and then excused herself. She was almost to the door, when she felt the hand on her arm.

Holly.

Her friend gazed up at her, with narrowed eyes that showed not the slightest trace of intoxication. "Be sure, Jillian," she said. "Be very careful."

"Being careful doesn't make a whole lot of sense just now, Holly."

Holly's calves bunched as she tiptoed up and kissed Jillian's cheek. Then she returned to her friends.

The back stairs were deserted, and Jillian raced down them, consumed now with an ugly curiosity. She slipped through the front door of dorm 7, then searched the registry until she found Mary's name.

Give them a little time. Let the sweet heavy intoxication of sex and alcohol, excitement and fatigue, work their savagely hypnotic magic.

For twenty minutes she stared sightlessly into Olympic Boulevard, eyes observing but not tracking the occasional tram. Then she dictated the number.

After a few seconds a drowsy, musically accented woman's voice came on the line. "Hello?"

"I have a message for your friend."

"Who is this?"

"I don't think names are important. Just give him the message."

A pause. Mary Ling's voice became cautious. "Yes?"

"The message is: the Denver Mountain Rescue committee would like to have a few words."

"Ah . . . I do not understand."

"That's all right. He will."

Almost exactly a minute later, Donny came on line. "Is this who I think it is?" His voice was more guarded than Mary's.

"Yes."

"Ah . . . listen. I'm sorry about the bad break that you got."

Go to hell. "Come and talk to me. I need five minutes."

He was down in four, wearing a robe that clung like wet silk. It was such a sight that she almost forgot what she came to say. She saw nervous impatience, but also a kind of arrogant compassion.

He said, "Listen, sorry about the way it went." His massive shoulders rippled the robe with his shrug. "There's nothing I can do about it."

"I know. I also know that it wouldn't be a good idea if anyone found out about your collapse on the mountainside."

The compassion went; so did the impatience. Easy arrogance now. The breeze shifted, and she caught a whiff of body oils, of Mary Ling's pungency. She was disgusted and utterly turned on at the same instant, and ashamed of her reaction. He watched her coolly. He said, "I wonder if you know what you're playing with."

"A little. I did some research. What's really going on here, Donny? Do a dying woman a favor."

Donny stopped, seemed to be listening to the wind. Finally, he sighed.

"I'll meet you up on the roof in ten minutes. Take the back stairs."

Jillian's ID card got her through the back door of dorm 7, and she climbed up the back stairs with legs and lungs and arms working together like gears churning in an implacable machine.

A chill wind whipped across the roof, but Jillian didn't feel it. She looked out across to the city lights.

Donny showed up fifteen minutes later.

He rubbed a wristband nervously. A weapon? More probably just a specialized comlink, something not patched directly into the neural net.

"So what do you want from me?"

"I want their *motives*. Is the Council at war with itself? Crime and plagues and civil disobedience and industrial accidents—I've seen work that could have stopped all that. They're *not* just accidents and happenstance and unavoidable turmoil."

"You're way out of your depth."

"I went through the public records. You've been representing Transportation, and Trans has been angling for a twelve percent increase in its rates shipping oil for Energy and Pan-Latin Industrial. Two days after the disruption of your nervous system, they settled for six and a half percent."

"I don't see—"

She was so tired of lies. The cityscape blurred in her vision. She closed her eyes, and the lights danced on her eyelids. "Sure you do, Donny. Within ten hours of your little problem, there were several 'events' involving your section leaders. A thrombosis in Bangkok. A myocardial infarction in Vienna. I counted twelve apparently unconnected events."

"Just where is this leading you, Jillian?"

"The Council is lying. They can't deliver on their promises. I'm not even sure they want to."

He turned up the collar on his robe. His face was hard. "I don't have anything to say to you. Your time is up."

"Donny—"

"Publish and be damned."

"No, no." She half laughed. "*They'd* never let me do that anyway, but Donny, I know about your illiteracy paper! It would have worked. We could have cut crime, human misery, violence. *They* chose not to. Why? And why did you let them buy you off?"

He stared at her, silent. He tried to twist away when she reached out to grasp his wrist, but her fingers dug in and held.

"The man who wrote that paper had compassion," she said urgently. "Insight. He cared, Donny. Look at yourself now. You don't believe in anything anymore. Did you know that your little bedmate *killed* Catherine St. Clair with a rock? Do you care?" It might have been her imagination, but Donny seemed to shiver. "What will you bet that nothing will be done about it? It isn't justice they're after, Donny. They want the best and the brightest to kill each other scrabbling to the top. They swallow our data whole, and use it or don't use it, but us they throw away. When they let someone like you through, you're a damned pet puppy.

"Tell me the truth, Donny. Make a dying woman happy."

A floatcar spun up into its flight pattern, the headlamps flashing across Donny. His handsome face was a mask of pain, of anger, of misery. After a long pause, he spoke.

"All right. The truth. But it won't make you happy, Jillian.

"It's *not* a war. A domination game, maybe. A few people die. Check the numbers on a single major battle in World War Two and tell me we're not better off. Everybody's better off."

"And the babies who die in poverty? Donny, if you can reduce crime and human misery by improving the schools, you can *increase* it by reducing the standard of education. How many little nudges has the Council used to weaken governments, destroy the faith of the voters, strengthen the corporations?"

"Jillian—"

"How much have you kept yourself from seeing, Donny? How about—Oh, my God."

"Conspiracy theories are old stuff. They can even be fun if you . . ." He saw her shock. "What?"

"Jesus Christ, I just saw it, just now. It's so blasted obvious once you think of it. Don't you see how the Council has been at war with the nations? They control the Olympiad. How many papers besides yours have been classified, Donny? For at least forty years the Council has had the best minds on the planet helping them undermine participatory government."

"Shit."

Jillian waited, but that was all Donny had to say. He believed her. It was *real*.

She asked, "Who's the Old Bastard, Donny?"

"I don't know," he said dully. "I've never seen him."

"It's a him? Not a her or a them?"

Donny shrugged. "The rumor is about an old man. The Council is waiting for him to die. He can't last much longer, they say. He's behind all of this. You want to blame someone, find *him*." He pulled his robe tight, and turned away from her. "Leave me alone,

Shomer. I don't want to know about any of this. I don't care what happens to you. Just . . . leave me to hell alone."

"You were the dream," she said contemptuously, stepping back away from him.

"I have to tell them we talked, dear heart. They'll know already, or they might. If they've been listening, you're dead. They don't need you, and if you're right about the nations . . . you're just dead." He shivered. "Goddamn you for telling me that."

"Donny Crawford." She spoke the name almost reverently. "I guess everyone dies in the Olympiad, huh, Donny?" She turned away abruptly.

"Goddamn you!"

But she was already dropping down the staircase, quick but quiet, in a fell-runner's controlled descent.

Chapter

14

Her body flamed with tension. Her instinct was to work it off.

She walked for half an hour, wanting to run but not wanting to be conspicuous, until chance brought her to the gymnasts' stadium.

The guards didn't stop her. The few workmen ignored her. She tried running, sprinting over and over around the indoor track until her legs and lungs burned and she was dizzy and nauseous with fatigue. From there she went to yoga, feeling the twists and turns clicking her spine into position effortlessly, handstanding, and bending herself into knots. She found a set of parallel bars, kipped up and spun into a series of free-form exercises that would have won a perfect ten only forty years ago. She was laughing, and crying.

Her body was perfect.

Her body was dying.

She was sweat-soaked and steaming when she left. An orange dawn caught her by surprise.

She was ravenous.

She found a restaurant just as it was opening. The waiter was smitten; she enjoyed that. She was the only customer. She ordered like an army battalion, and watched the waiter's jaw sag.

For all of this time she was wondering how she would die.

The Council would know of her conversation with Donny. They might know now . . . or not; they couldn't monitor every conversation on planet Earth. But because they *might* know, Donny would tell them.

They couldn't afford to allow her to live.

Someone would come for her. Or a car would crash. Or botulism would develop in her food. *My God, have I really eaten that much?* She was pleasantly full, with just room for more coffee. And she might as well enjoy herself, because it seemed she was out of answers.

If she could tell the people . . .

But *They* controlled the media. No message would get out.

. . . Beverly's last message. *It is theoretically possible for a single human being to control fifty-four percent of world economic activity, forty-eight percent of political activity . . .*

But Beverly had been talking about the Old Bastard. Any Council member would control much less.

The media *could not* be perfectly controlled.

. . . Close enough, though, probably. (They hadn't used the botulism yet. She felt wonderful. She was even getting used to Greek coffee.) What would she have to do to get a message out? Hijack a video station?

A family of six drifted in. Could these . . . no. The four boys were suspiciously well behaved, but still too young to be professional assassins.

—Hijack a spacecraft. She could use it to control a relay satellite and *really* blanket the world with her story.

The restaurant wasn't hers anymore, so she left. She ran two miles along the strand, on wet sand, sprinting backward, passing other runners as if they were jogging through quicksand.

—Murder Mary Ling. That'd get media attention!

Beginning to puff now, she passed a lean runner and grinned back at him. He took it as an invitation and chased her. He was good, she was beginning to tire, and she faced forward and put some effort into it. She led him into a subway entrance, where he gave up.

She took the subway back to her hotel.

She stretched out on the bed and wondered if she would sleep. Or wake up.

—The vicious little rock-throwing bitch hadn't trained as a fighter. Strangle her in public! Surrender immediately, then talk to anyone and everyone, tell every secret, announce always that the Council is bound to have Jillian Shomer murdered. When it finally happens, it'll confirm everything.

Actually, it might work.

That was disturbing.

Jillian had been raised Episcopal; her faith had never flagged. She had considered tracking and killing her mother's murderer . . . but her mother had been killed by a social pattern. Vengeance required breaking the pattern. But not murder! Surely her conscience would never tempt her to so great a sin.

Or to suicide; but last night she'd been close.

So look again. The Council's dominance games have brought death and misery to hundreds of thousands of people. Killing one innocent to break that pattern still cannot be justified; but Mary Ling is no innocent. Her public strangling would buy the attention Jillian needed. The media would be hot to watch a hair-pulling match between two Olympic contenders. Especially if they were supposed to be fighting over a man, over Donny Crawford.

—Tell every secret: *that* was the flaw. *They* had cut her off from her data. Without Holly Lakein's help she would have nothing. If she exposed Holly, Holly would die, too.

Jillian was almost relieved.

—Hold it. Let the media believe that she'd used her own data sources! Granted that the Council had silenced Beverly; but who would ever tell?

The wall pulsed, and buzzed gently.

This was actually getting to be fun; she didn't appreciate the interruption. "Yes?"

A man's face appeared on the wall. She had never seen it before, but he was young, and pleasant, and officious. "Good morning. I'm Stewart Kaporov at Olympiad Central. Would you please report to our offices? There has been a slight irregularity."

Too late. She'd never had a plan anyway.

For an instant she considered fleeing; but her face was known everywhere on Earth. She considered going as she was. Instead she took a quick shower, rinsed a mealy taste out of her mouth, and tried to do something nice with her hair.

Her whole body was beginning to cramp. She set out for the nearest subway entrance.

The streets were curiously deserted now, wistfully so. A few young men and women in silver blazers hustled here and there, and workmen were disassembling platforms and collapsing temporary scaffolding.

There was a nice, busy, alive sound in the air.

The subway was crowded. It must have been unbelievable during the games; it was the reason none of the contenders had tried it. An elderly gentleman offered her his seat; she refused with a smile.

The offices of Olympiad Central were in the Arts and Entertainments pavilion, and the guard at the front entrance recognized her and opened it at once, saying "Third floor, Miss Shomer."

She nodded without speaking, walking straight to the elevators, giving him a clean shot at her back.

Larry Niven & Steven Barnes

Nothing. She reached the elevator, and it *bing'd* and opened at once.

Where is Mary Ling, she wondered, *right now*?

The ride to the third floor was surprisingly uneventful. No cyanide, no sudden stall. No Ninjas dropping from the roof. A genuine smile curled her mouth at that image. She chuckled, a good sound.

Kaparov's secretary ushered Jillian into a spacious office. A wall-wide vidscreen showed waves rolling peacefully in from the Aegean.

Kaporov entered, and stopped, and seemed to brace himself. He looked threatened, here in his own office. "Miss Shomer?"

"So far."

"Ah . . . yes. Well. We have a . . . difficult situation here."

"Yes."

"I believe you know Miss Osa Grevstad."

"Of course."

"There was a . . . diplomatic problem. The papers which allowed her to compete on North American Agricorp were never completely validated. She has lost her position. Considering the fact that your loss to her in judo cost you five points, you are now in position for the gold as opposed to the silver."

Jillian was frozen, couldn't even react when he extended his hand. Just like that. Could it really be that simple? Could they . . .

Oh God. Osa? The ultraconfident, brutally skilled strangler had just been given the death sentence. Because of Jillian.

She couldn't take the gold. And yet . . .

If she didn't, and the judgment on Osa's status had already been announced, what good would she have done?

Jillian extended a trembling hand.

"Congratulations," he said.

15

It took nearly forty-five minutes to push through the reporters and the crowds at Kennedy Airport. It was all a smiling, churning mob.

In twos and threes, the Olympians were hustled into cars. She caught sight of Donny talking to a phalanx of reporters. His smile seemed just as warm and sincere as ever. His gaze slid across her without stopping to focus.

She was ushered into a car with the Bulgarian Gilbert and Sullivan devotee. They waved at the crowd like newlyweds.

Once the car started moving, she closed her eyes and leaned back into her seat. The long-postponed fatigue came crashing down on her. Or else it was emotional whiplash from the changes in her life . . . or jet lag . . . or the beginning of the death that comes with Boost.

In a few days there would be another operation. She would be one of the Linked then, part machine, and death would no longer be inevitable. Death would come when she lost a dominance game . . . whose rules she had better learn quickly.

The Bulgarian put his hand on Jillian's arm. "Your name is Jillian?"

She turned.

"I am Jorge."

His square face was too close; his elbows and knees occupied too much of the space. He was one of the runners, tall and attenuated. Folding him into the car had been awkward. Any second now he'd go *Sproing!* and pop through both doors.

He grew tired of waiting for a response. "We don't know each other, but we will both be Linked now. Special people we are." He grinned infectiously, and she thought of Sean, lost love, left a world away. "Perhaps we could spend some time . . ."

Her smile was broken from overuse. She said, "I think we both need rest."

It sounded stupid; small wonder if he didn't take the hint. "Soon. We are both staying at the MGM Grand Hotel?"

The car had stopped for a traffic light. Jillian opened the car door and stepped out. To the astonished Bulgarian she said, "Later. Sorry."

She just couldn't face any more *faces*.

The traffic was moving again. She wove her way

to the curb in a blare of horns, stepping on bumpers, vaulting over hoods, swinging across an overhead rail. She was too tired to word-dance with a man on the make; but not too tired for fell-running in traffic.

Did she *have* to go to the MGM Grand? Her luggage would be going there, and she'd need a phone to get a reservation elsewhere. She would regret her rudeness later. Send him flowers? Ask him to dinner and apologize? She might need Jorge as an ally. She looked about her for a subway entrance.

*   *   *

The old concrete had taken on a thousand different shades. Time and travelers had worn ruts in the floor. The shops, gates, ticket dispensers, and barber booths varied from sparkling new through venerable to decrepit. The lighting was uneven; one could imagine muggers in the shadows.

Parts of H. P. Lovecraft's "Dream Quest" had been filmed in these ancient tunnels, ten years before Jillian was born. Those were the scenes where Carter lived among the ghouls.

Jillian used her credit disk to summon food from a noodle dispenser. She ate while she unraveled the maps on the walls. These days she seemed to be hungry all the time.

She wanted platform 28, an L car. Just get her luggage, find another hotel, and *go*.

It was deep in the bowels of the earth, down an escalator that seemed to run all the way to Hell. New York's subways had a bad old reputation. Charles

Bronson and Bernhard Goetz no longer sprinted up and down the escalators . . . but their prey, the muggers, were gone too, and Jillian Shomer could break any ancient mugger in four pieces without working up a hunger.

The platform was occupied. A little girl held her mother's hand. The girl was maybe eight years old and small for her age, all in pleated cotton print. She had long red hair that might never have been cut at all, falling past her shoulders in a scarlet cascade. She looked at Jillian for three minutes, while a score more of passengers gathered and avoided each other's eyes. Finally the little girl screwed up her courage.

'' 'Scuse me,'' she said politely. ''Aren't you Jill Shomer?''

Jillian smiled, and gave a small nod. The girl's mother glanced sideways a little, gave a quick, nervous smile, and stared straight ahead.

A gleaming silver tube six cars long emerged from the tunnel with a silent puff of air. Four cars were marked as L's.

The little redhead's eyes never moved from Jillian's. ''I saw you on the vid,'' she said worshipfully. ''When I grow up, I'm going to be an Olympian! I want to be just like you.''

Jillian's smile drooped.

The cars opened. The girl's mother dragged her toward a front car. The redhead waved frantically. Jillian turned to find a less crowded car, and locked eyes with a tall, wiry man with square-cut brown hair and a florid complexion.

Sean!

Sean Vorhaus gaped. Then he waved, pointed, and half ran for the last L car.

Jillian followed, already becoming irritated. He could have waited! These cars came through every fifteen minutes. How did *he* know they both wanted a local? And what was he doing *here*, and why hadn't he told her? Oh, maybe there was a message waiting for her at the blasted MGM Grand—

There were six people in the car, with seats for at least twenty. Weird. A moment ago it was as crowded as the others. Sean must be at the back. She'd *thought* he was at the back—

The doors had closed.

These little airtight cylinders were in use worldwide. They ran on independent motors and switched back and forth from train to train, from locals to gravity-assisted cross-continental vacuum tubes to tunnels that ran beneath the oceans—and they were too small to hide in. Where was Sean?

She'd missed him somehow, and the other six passengers were staring at her. She sat down next to an old Hispanic woman. Now only a chubby late-teen in loose creased pants, white shirt, and a vest sweater was still looking at her. She waited for the 38th Street platform.

The train hummed along in near silence. The dim light fluttered a little when the car reached its first switch point. The train slowed. The cars decoupled, and rearranged with cars from other lines, clicking back together and heading down new lines.

There was an odd bulge in the boy's sweater, like a small left breast. The kid was soft, undermuscled, overpadded. His eyes flicked toward her every few moments. Wearily she thought, *Again?*

The car dropped. Jillian stifled a scream of surprise. There was a soft *pop*. They'd passed a seal, into vacuum. The car was still falling, still accelerating. But this was a local line! They shouldn't have—

Alarmed, she glanced at the other passengers. They were taking it very well, suspiciously well. None of them had moved. In fact . . . they were fewer.

They were disappearing whenever she turned her head!

Now only the kid in the sweater was left.

The car was still falling through the Earth.

Jillian made herself relax as Abner had taught her. If *They* wanted to kill her, there were a thousand easier ways . . . and her fear of death, she discovered, was gone. Clean gone.

She asked, ''Are you a hologram, too?'' He had to be. She was getting her first good look. Wrinkles in his pants. Buttons, zippers, *glasses*—He must be as old as the subways.

The kid smiled back at her. ''I'm the Old Bastard,'' he said.

Chapter

16

She asked, "What's that on your chest?"

Of the myriad questions whirling through her head, she'd found one to surprise him. His smile flickered. Then he pulled his sweater over his head. There was a pocket in his rumpled shirt, and a clear plastic envelope in the pocket, and a dozen colored sticks in that.

"Shirt protector."

"What's in it?"

"Things for writing and drawing. These days I'd have a wrist link, or just use the neural net. Ever see one of these?" He pulled, from a pants pocket that couldn't have been deep enough, a flat wooden stick painted white with fine black markings. "My father had one. Slide rule."

Larry Niven & Steven Barnes

She remembered: a slide rule came somewhere between an abacus and a pocket calculator. "That must be worth a fortune."

Almost unconsciously, her hand had drifted out toward it. Her "ghost" snatched it out of reach in a gesture reminiscent of a ten-year-old protecting a sheaf of trading chits. A sheepish smile. "Let's save some time, Jillian. The Council doesn't know about this interview and never will. The car is headed for Denver. So's your luggage. The records will show you arranged it all yourself. Half the passengers in another car are listed as traveling on *this* car. So we've got plenty of time to solve any little mysteries that are still bothering you, but let's not abuse it, okay? I need some of my attention for the rest of the planet."

Jillian examined the Old Bastard, seeing too much weakness. The thin shoulders, the baggy body, the eager, friendly eyes. This was the monster who controlled the Council? She felt disorientation, savage disappointment, and an almost morbid distaste.

She said, "You arranged for my gold, didn't you?"

"Yes."

"You've killed Osa."

"Osa bribed her way in. Not likely to pass her genes on, either. She'll try again in four years."

"And Abner."

"Because of our research, Abner lived long enough to coach you."

She paused. "And my mother?"

"She was in the wrong place at the wrong time."

"Accident?"

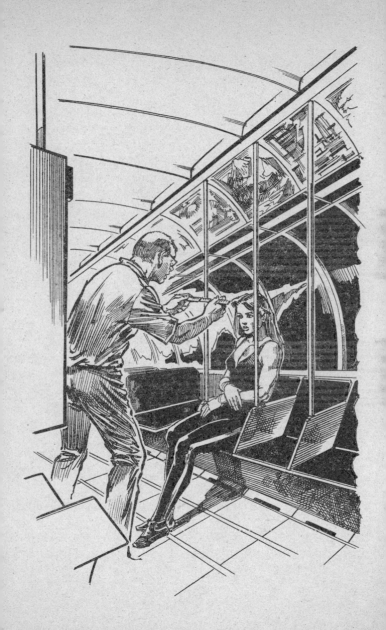

"Jillian, it's the kind of accident that happens when things aren't running right. Mining and Agricorp were dancing. Certain machines didn't get serviced. A program picked up some noise. A waldo claw picked up just the top of a habitat when . . . sorry." The boy flickered and was in a different position, palms raised in supplication. "Calm down, Jillian. Maybe I'm giving you this too fast—"

Her voice trembled, rose to a half-scream. "Just tell me *why.*"

"I can't do that short."

"Long, then."

He nodded once. "It's been an even century since I looked like this. Computer nerds, they called us. We didn't get along well with people, but we got along fine with computers.

"Computers don't deal in nuances. If I type, 'Is there no friend to rid me of this pestilential priest?' my computer doesn't kill Thomas à Becket for me. It says, 'Bad command or file name' and waits for me to say what I mean. Sanskrit was one of the few spoken languages with no ambiguity. Using it produced a useful clarity of thought, and birthed a body of philosophy. Computer programmers speak a language of mathematics. When that language became integrated into our natural thought patterns, it was the beginning of an entirely new human culture, Jillian."

"Capable of mastering the world?"

"Capable, with the eventual development of Linkage, of mastering our own nervous systems."

Jillian wanted to laugh. "It doesn't seem to have helped Donny. You still have wars."

He brushed it off. "I'll get to that. You still listening?"

He waited for her nod.

"We learned computers," he said. "We made computers and programs. Some of us used computer power to keep track of the stock market—" He saw her eyebrows arch. "It tracked the worldwide flow of wealth. Often you can move wealth to where it's worth more. Some of us got rich. Some played politics. Around nine hundred of us took *major* risks, played with our brains and bodies, linked ourselves directly to infrared and UV sensors, satellite broadcasts, digital telescopes and microscopes, computer memory, data sources like the stock exchange and traffic monitors and police bands, and of course we developed our own."

"And you turn geniuses into weaklings. You kill innocent people."

This time he ignored her. "Some died. Some went Feral. Eighty of us had control of most of the world's wealth before we came into serious conflict. Eleven of us are left, and another eighteen who came later, and we constitute the Council. But as for war, it's more like a quarrel at a bridge club—"

"You must have killed thousands of people by now!"

"You're misusing the word, but it's not your fault. We've altered the records." For an instant he looked haggard. "After you're Linked, spend an hour reading about *war*. You'll have access to the reality. The death rate could be *millions*."

She didn't want to think about that at *all*. She said, "You don't really call yourself the Old Bastard."

"I call myself Saturn. You could hunt up my original name, but it wouldn't tell you much."

Saturn? Leave it. "What do you look like now?"

Then she jumped. There was a great oval bed in the car with them; its far edge was beyond where the tramcar's wall should have been. Its surface rolled in slow shallow waves, a sluggish ocean, as if the bed were more alive than the patient. Machinery hovered above the bed, fading above the tramcar's roof, extending thick umbilicals that bifurcated repeatedly to cover the patient in a fur of silver spiderweb.

That impossibly ancient figure seemed to be part man, part machine. Just as she decided that the thing must be dead, its head popped up and slurred, "Did you ever see a movie called *Two-Thousand-One*? Eh, eh," and fell back.

The kid said earnestly, "That's me. Barely. It's the pattern that's important, and the pattern is in the bubbles . . . recorded in bubble memory," he amplified before she could say, *Huh?*

"So why not kill the thing?"

The old man's head lifted again. It spoke with mushy difficulty. "Here I have senses I don't have elsewhere. Smell. Memory. Shtuff that's hard to retrieve, but imposh—impossible to copy over. I don't mean I can't make it work. I mean, impossible."

"Saturn. Are you still human?"

The ancient smiled; the boy spoke. "Very good, Jillian. But leave it for a moment, okay?" Again he'd answered instantly. He never stopped to think.

His holographic appearance was older than she had originally thought. Twenty-five? His posture: he was *not* awkward, *not* diffident, *not* watching a desirable woman and praying she wouldn't notice. He leaned forward, looking directly into her eyes, challenging, good smile lines at the corners of his mouth.

Jillian said, "Okay. There are problems the Council doesn't solve. Crime. Disaster control. Safety designs. We could make Paradise, and I'm not the only Olympic contender who's proved it. Saturn, what's wrong with Paradise?"

"Wrong problem."

"Then *why did Lilith Shomer die*?"

He said, "A small group of people can control an entire world. Can evaluate a trillion bytes of data without a moment's personal experience. Can reduce people, animals, plants, whole populations and ecologies to integers to be manipulated. The Council does that."

"Nobody cared enough?"

"That's part of it. Jillian, it is *very* tempting."

"Why aren't you tempted?"

For the first time, Saturn broke eye contact with her. "If you look at a human being as a machine," he said softly, "as a stimulus-response loop, what happens when every urge can be met with a trickle of electricity? When fantasies are as powerful as reality? The world . . . *your* world is no more real than what's in the bubbles . . . what happens in my own mind. Megalomania and catatonia are very real companions to the Link. That's the rest of the problem, Jillian. Citizens die when we go Feral."

"Oh."

"I give Donny five years."

"And the rest of humanity?"

"That's up to you, Jillian."

Now it was Jillian's turn to be silent.

"Why me?" she asked finally. "What is this all about? And what makes you any different?"

"I created the game. And when I Linked, and lived more in the machine than in my body, and could create or reexperience every sensation imaginable, I thought I would be happy."

"And you weren't?"

"No, and it frightened me. If you have everything, and the hunger still exists, then the hunger has nothing to do with stimulus and response. The answer doesn't lie in the realm of objective reality *or* subjective experience. It has to do with the function of the observing mind in the creation of its world. Jillian, who is the 'I' that sees and desires?"

"That . . .," she said carefully, "is a very old question."

"And a very new one. Am I really in the bubbles? We need an answer. For the first time in human history, we can have literally anything that we want, including immortality . . . and the Linked are proving that it's not enough. We wage petty power-game wars. Homicidal intrigue. We totter into insanity. It's the furthest reach of human technology and experience, and it might be a dead end."

Perhaps for dramatic effect, the light had shifted to highlight Saturn. She noticed that the bed was gone, patient, machinery and all. Saturn was a sensitive host.

Jillian said, "You thought you were a machine, didn't you?"

Saturn nodded quietly.

"That's why you buried yourself in a world of mathematics. In retrospect, it makes sense that the whole thing is coming apart."

Again, the almost imperceptible dip of the chin.

"But you still dream, don't you, Saturn? You still desire? You think you should be free of the flesh, of all this, and you're not, and you don't know what to make of it."

The tube car was silent, save for a distant hiss of air through the ventilation system. "I have access to all the information in the world," he said. "And I can't answer that question."

"Where do I come in? Do I? Is it that you want to be told that you have a soul?"

He waved it away. "*You* can't answer that question. This isn't about me, Jillian—"

"Isn't it? Has it ever been about anything else?"

"It's about saving humanity—"

"Which you are a part of, like it or not."

He glared at her. "I deal in what is quantifiable, Jillian. I never wonder how many angels can dance on the head of a pin—that question being, incidentally, an exercise in quantum mechanics—"

"I'm not interested in a lecture," she said flatly.

"Jillian, shall I turn up the heat?"

"Please." Quite suddenly, she was freezing. And he'd known before she did!

"Done. I wonder," he said, "if you realize how many ways there are to be human. Maoris, Nazis, Mormons, abos in the Australian outback, slaves and slavers, drug cultures in the United States in the sixties and then the eighties, don't even *start* to cover it. There are all the dead cultures, too. The French and Soviet reigns of terror. Ancient half-humans who ate shellfish and each other. Mental hospitals. Christian sects wherein the men castrated themselves. Rosicrucians. The Velvet Underground.

"You could take most of the aliens in science fiction and match their lifestyles to *somebody*. I remember a critic who thought Bram Stoker's *Dracula* was about syphilis. Or take Ursula Le Guin's—"

"I haven't—"

"You did, too. Third year of high school, English Lit. You wrote a paper, 'Vampirism as a Venereal Metaphor.' It was quite explicit, and led to what you described to your diary as an 'affair of incandescent intensity, sufficient to set the moon ablaze' with your Lit tutor." He grinned happily, an innocent voyeur. "You read Le Guin, too."

Her face was burning. "How dare you! Do you think peeping into the emotions of real human beings makes you more alive? You're a ghoul, Saturn. You don't even have the courage to lie down and die." She felt violated. Saturn had pried into Beverly! He must know everything, every hope and prayer, every childhood memory. How *could* he?

"Are we done? Le Guin, *The Left Hand of Darkness*. Le Guin's aliens are a branch of the human race, but they're neuter most of the time, and when they develop a gender you can't guess which one—" She remembered then, and he saw it. "Okay. Good science fiction, but do you think I can't find people like that in Oakland?

"But the other side is, whenever I wonder about

213

something, it starts a subprogram. I've got access to most of human knowledge.

"Twenty-six years ago I wondered if I was human. I had an answer with ninety-one percent confidence in just under two minutes. In ten minutes I had four nines of confidence. Every known human culture had been explored. Le Guin's aliens were human, Dracula was human, but by any reasonable standard, I'm not."

"Imagine my surprise," Jillian said bitterly.

"Rise above it, Jillian. More is at stake here than your feelings."

"They're what make me human!"

"Having them, or wallowing in them? I thought you prized discipline. Strength. Achievement. Emotional control makes it possible. Do you see the implications of what I said? Maybe the Council's not human, either?"

"So you keep replacing them. Your children. *Saturn.*"

"You got it."

"How long? Until you get it *right*?"

"I'm getting closer. The younger Linked are staying human longer. I need to keep them under control, too. You spoke of motives. I don't trust theirs. Mine you must have guessed—No? All right, Jillian, what would you do if you were me?"

She felt bone-weary. It was all too much, too quick. Her head was reeling, and she yawned mightily. "Sleep for a week."

"Coffee under the seat. Jillian, I can't do this twice. The Council can see patterns. I won't make you a target, Jillian. This conversation ends at Denver."

Fair enough.

Under the seat was a wrinkled plastic bag. It held a small thermos and a Bullocks sales slip and a package of oat bran cookies with several missing. *My God, he's thorough.* The coffee was black and sweet, not too hot. She could feel it pulling her awake.

She said, "Kill them all and then suicide." She surprised herself that time: there wasn't any bitterness in that suggestion.

Again Saturn answered instantly. "What about the equipment? Software, computers, never-linked sensing devices, tailored medical procedures like Boost, everything that made us what we are: what about *that*? If the capability is there, there will be more Linked."

"That . . . *that's* why the new stuff stopped appearing in the shops!"

"Yes, that was me."

"Mph. You could destroy . . . How far back would we have to go to be safe? Nineteen fifty?"

"Destroy the information?" Saturn shrugged. "Making transistors disappear may be beyond me. No, that's not the way to go. I want a human being who can use everything that was and is available to me, and still remain human. What do I have to do to accomplish that?"

"You'd have to . . . a training program? You son of a bird. You changed the Olympics."

"Yes. To help me find people like you, or shape them. Mind and body and spirit. I had to make some compromises, but that won't last. One day a majority of the Council will be Olympic winners. *They* won't put up with the current death rate. Will *you*?"

Will *I*. "Not likely. What have you got in mind?"

"Change the rules. Even so, the pattern I'm looking for includes courage. I get that through the Olympics. I'm trying other approaches too. Give computer equipment to primitives after they reach fifty. Gene carving—"

"Only a monster of arrogance would decide what constitutes *human*."

"Give me a human and I'll let him rewrite my specs! *I* don't dare. Jillian, the Link techniques are too good. They must be used. The Linked will *be* the human race. They're a wall across the future, even if they're a blind alley. If they go Feral and rip up the Earth, that's the future too. If they can stay human—I just need *one*."

"To be your . . . child?"

"Partner. Successor. You're too filled with doubt, Jillian. Power won't turn you into a monster. It may kill you, tear you apart, but you're no stranger to inner conflict. I think you'd say that was part of your birthright as a human being, wouldn't you?"

She was silent.

"Wouldn't you say it was a natural result of the soul's attempt to achieve perfection in human form? Wouldn't you tell me of Christ's temptation in the desert, his despair on the cross?"

"Shut up," Jillian said flatly. "Just shut up. Don't mock me, Saturn. If you don't believe in the human soul, then you don't know who I am, no matter how many facts you may have stored away."

"You have friends who aren't Christian. You won't demand that I convert."

Fair enough. But—"What do you want from me, Saturn?"

"Not much. I protected you when you were using Holly Lakein to get information. I've put you among the Linked. You'll be one of the powers that rule the human race, on the Earth and off—"

"You've made this speech before."

"To all who'd listen. To the others I'm the old one, the crazy one."

"You're not offering much, either, are you?"

"I don't interfere with the dominance games, no. You'll be on your own, and I'll be watching, hoping you can become what I'm hoping to see. If you make it, then welcome to the human race. A small, select group."

She stared at him. He waited . . . probably busy elsewhere, a hundred elsewheres, leaving a tendril of attention for the hologram in the subway car.

She sipped coffee, and thought.

She no longer feared death . . . she had finally accepted that she need not. What she feared now was that she would become Saturn.

Presently she said, "Here it is, Saturn, like it or not. You could have gone to six decimal points, or twenty, and it wouldn't make any difference. What it is to be human can't be determined by what we were. Human evolution is too sensitive to initial conditions. My religion says that we bring something into this life which is beyond flesh, or mind, or emotion. I can't prove it, you can't disprove it. I choose to believe it. I think that you're so totally human you scare yourself. You look at me and say, 'Ah, she has the humanity I gave up,' and it's a crock. Your brain is alive. Your heart is asleep. Wake up, damn you. You may be the only chance we have.''

She held her breath for a long beat. Saturn was motionless. Five seconds, perhaps. How many worlds of possibility did he spin through in that moment? Was he reviewing the entirety of his life? Or a thousand futures, projecting fractal probabilities to the nth power?

Then he sighed, and smiled timidly. Saturn held out an ethereal hand to her.

''God help me.''

''Help us both,'' Saturn said.

Was he mocking her? She couldn't tell. She must trust him until she learned more.

She extended her hand. There was no sensation of touch or pressure, just a man's hand melting into hers, sealing a bargain whose implications she was just beginning to consider. Then she was alone, falling beneath the earth at three miles per second.

The cab dropped Jillian Shomer off at the main gate of the Rocky Mountain Sports Medicine Facility. She stood there surrounded by three bags of luggage. The air carried a strong chill, and she tugged her collar up.

The gate slowly slid back, welcoming her.

Once there was a woman named Lilith Shomer.

Jillian hefted the bags in her hands and across her shoulders, over a hundred pounds total. She barely felt the weight. She began to walk toward the Medtech facility, a gleaming dome which flamed in the noonday sun.

The new Comnet wristlink still felt odd. She preferred the earpieces: at least she could take them off. From this point onward, the Council would know where she was at every moment, who she was with, what they said, what they did.

The price of immortality was privacy. How could it be otherwise? Her body must be monitored from outside; it could no longer run itself.

She had a little girl named Jillian, and died, an innocent victim of a secret war.

The external camp was deserted. Soon, perhaps within weeks, the first arrivals would begin anew. Training for a winter Olympics still three years distant. A new, young, hopeful multitude would begin to climb that fatal, irresistible peak once again.

The little girl grew up to be a woman who lived a dream of honor and responsibility, and had that dream corrupted—

She stopped, watching the rays of sunlight reflected from the dome. If she squinted just a bit, the lines of light seemed to fracture off into finer and finer lines.

—so many choices, so many possible futures. And every new day closes a billion options and opens a billion more. Lives are sensitive to initial conditions.

She set the luggage down, and removed an identification card from her pocket, waited for the door to ask her name, for her palm print, for her retinal scan.

When it did, and opened to her, she carried her baggage in. A silver-vested attendant took it, gleaming a cap-toothed smile at her. ''Room 110-A, Miss Shomer. They'll be with you in a while. You're early.''

''Yes,'' she said quietly.

In an hour the doctors would be ready for her. They would begin preliminaries for the Linking operation. She had needed terribly to arrive early, to have time to think, and to hear her own thoughts in peace.

And would they be Jillian's thoughts at this time next week? Could one be a god, and human, too?

Room 110-A opened to her touch. She sat in a small theater looking down on the operating room. A place of conference, perhaps. Of meditation and strengthening of resolve.

In the white-tiled room beneath her, her skull would be opened once again, and new life breathed into her.

She folded her hands around her face, biting her lip until pain rang in her head. She wouldn't cry. She wouldn't.

What price privacy? Saturn certainly had ways of maintaining his privacy. Perhaps there was a way to write fiction into what her Comnet sent to the Council. She had better learn how.

After a time, her wristlink buzzed. Jillian wearily touched it to an intercom on the seat in front of her, and a throat/earpiece popped out of a slot. She slid it into place. Fog washed across the seat in front of her, and then it was a window.

The man in the window was crested like a bird, in silver. It was the first thing she noticed: a fatly curved metal ridge, three or four pounds from the look of it, ran from his forehead to halfway down the back of his head, to where tightly coiled white hair was still growing.

"Jillian Shomer!" he said merrily.

"Yes." Too heavy for comfort. Could it be silvered plastic? Its proud obtrusiveness *had* to make him a

Council member. He looked to be in his sixties, in good health given a sedentary lifestyle; and *that* would make him one of the second generation, after Saturn but previous to the altered Olympics.

"I'm Carter McFairlaine. Transportation."

"Pleased to meet you."

"Well, well. I know that Arts and Entertainments is bidding for your services, but I wanted to have lunch with you next week to discuss the advantages of a Transportation contract."

After you Link, and you are ours.

"I'd be—" His head turned for an instant, to something offstage, and back. She saw the socket at the back end of the crest. Her breath caught. She understood with her guts, then: *He's part machine!*

"—delighted," she finished.

"Fine." That gleeful look: he'd caught her reaction. "I'll put the appointment into your personal data system. Beverly, I think her name is?"

"I . . . *what*?!"

McFairlaine chuckled. "Welcome to the team." And he faded out—

—and was replaced almost immediately by another face.

The coppery strands were more pronounced in Beverly's hair now. The cheekbones somehow softer, the mouth gentler. But it was Beverly, and Jillian's first, frighteningly powerful urge was to say to hell with the Linking operation and just jump into her Void that moment.

She dared not, not yet. Beverly had been edited.

Jillian reached out to touch the holoscreen, her fin-

gers disappearing into depth before brushing flat plastic. "Beverly."

"Who else, sugar?"

"I was so worried . . ."

"You're getting to be a popular girl. I put through that last call, but starting next week, you've got appointments lined up from here to Memphis." Beverly cocked her head slightly, gave Jillian a shrewdly appraising gaze. "Is there something I should know about, hon?"

"You will, in time."

"I notice they're piping me in over the priority network. Executives, rich folks, and Linked only—" Beverly stopped, and her mouth was an O of surprise. "Persons unknown have updated me, two seconds ago. I'll be—You lost and then you won! Jillian, why can't you do things like other people do?"

"I don't seem to be like other people . . ." Her fingers scratched against the plastic like a kitten pawing at a porch screen, trying to get into a warm house. "Please, Beverly. Don't go on at me. I missed you so much."

"Missed me? I haven't been anywhere. You don't call, you don't write, sometimes I think you just don't love me anymore—" Beverly locked up for a moment, because Jillian was crying.

She couldn't help it now. Tears were spilling from her eyes and both palms were pressed against the holoscreen, buried in Beverly's face.

"I haven't seen you cry for eleven years, darlin'," Beverly said softly. "Shhh. I'm here with you. I'll always be here. You've got to help me understand what you need, and I'll be that for you. You know that."

There were sounds in the building around her. A three-man medical tech team entered the operating room below her, led by a thin, efficient-looking Chinese man who began to check the instruments with sober thoroughness.

"Beverly. You—" *Go look for the Old Bastard. Make contact with him. Partition off, and find out everything that you can . . .*

She couldn't tell Beverly that. It would be suicide, until they could slip into a Void together. Honesty, like so many other things, would have to wait.

The men down in the operating theater looked up at her, motioned her to come down. Talk. And then Preop. And then . . .

"Beverly. I have to go now. I'll be back."

"I'm sure you will."

"I have promises to keep."

"And miles to go before you sleep?"

"Yes." Jillian smiled. "Miles. Good night, Beverly."

"Good night, Jillian. Sweet dreams."

The screen winked off.

Lives, Jillian thought, *are like weather, are sensitive to initial conditions. And because of that, not Comnet, or the Old Bastard, or the Council . . .*

Especially *the Council*.

. . . could predict lives.

New, from
Larry Niven's
forthcoming collection,

*PLAYGROUNDS
OF THE MIND*

THE PORTRAIT OF
DARYANREE THE KING

It was a good game while it lasted. Jovan left the
palace that night as a hunted fugitive, ruined by the
mannerless sixteen-year-old daughter of a border
nobleman; but at noon he had joined His Majesty's
Thirty-Eighth Birthday Celebration as one of the
most powerful men in Seaclaw.

The parades and games made pleasant cover for
the real business of the Birthday, as two hundred local
and visiting nobles gathered to meet anyone who could
do them good. By sunset all was circles of private
conversation; an outsider might as well go home. The
guests had eaten well and drunk better. King Daryanree
was monopolizing the youthful Lady Silvara, to the dis-
comfiture of many who coveted her attention, or his.

Larry Niven

Jovan should have been watching them. But he had made an ill-considered remark to Raskad Mil, and the princes' brass-voiced teacher had backed him against a wall to lecture on ghosts.

Jovan was flattered but wary. Old Mil had taught literature and history to the king as well as to his sons. He was treating Jovan as an equal. That could help Jovan's own reputation . . . unless Mil caught the purported artist-magician in some egregious ignorance.

"I only said that I had never seen one," he protested.

Mil would have none of that. "After all, where do barbarous peoples bury their dead? The ancient battlefields become the graveyards, do they not? And so they remain centuries later. You, Jovan, you hail from a war-torn land. Of course you see no ghosts!"

A young man at Jovan's shoulder asked the question Jovan dared not. "Why would it matter, Raskad Mil? Battlefields—"

"Ancient wars were fought with magic as well as swords. The sites are exhausted of the *manna*, the magical force. Ghosts give no trouble on a battlefield."

"But—"

"But Seaclaw's battles were all at sea, and even that was long ago. Our folk have always buried their dead on Worm's-Head Hill, with a view of land and sea for their comfort."

They were superstitious, the Seaclaw folk. Jovan's smile slipped when peals of laughter suddenly rang through the audience hall. He'd missed something—

Conversation stopped. Lady Silvara was easily the loveliest women in the hall; but she was young and fresh from the border, untrained in courtly ways. In the silence her voice was clear, musical. "Majesty, I would have thought that a man of your age would find interest in less strenuous pursuits!"

The King's fury showed only for an instant. Give him credit, King Daryanree had learned self-control at the negotiation tables. He said, "But unlike many a lovely young lady, Silvara, I grow no older."

And Jovan was already working his way through the crowd, not hurrying, but *moving*. He barely heard Silvara's, "Dyeing one's hair does nothing for crows'-feet, Majesty—"

At the great doors Jovan nodded to the guards and passed outside. A sliver of sun still showed at the northern edge of Worm's-Head Hill. An autumn chill was setting in. While an attendant went for Jovan's cloak, another stepped into the courtyard and waved peremptorily toward the line of coaches. Nothing moved. The attendant said, "Councillor, I don't see your driver."

Jovan knew about luck. Like wine: when luck turns sour, the whole barrel is sour. "Kassily probably went for a drink. Well, it's a nice night for a walk."

"We can provide you with a coachman—"

"No, I'll just go on down to the World-Turtle

Larry Niven

and send Kassily back for the coach." Jovan waited. Death for the price of a cloak? He could not leave without it. In this cold he would seem freakish.

The man returned with Jovan's cloak, and Jovan wished them both goodnight and strolled off into the growing dark.

Now what?

In any place that knew him, the King's men could find him. The King would be wanting explanations! Jovan had known that this might come. For eight years he had postponed his departure. The King might die, some fool might steal the painting for its powers; at worst he could be clear before the King's hairline began to recede; and meanwhile his wealth accumulated in Rynildissen.

Jovan turned left toward the World-Turtle, toward the sea, toward Seaclaw's ancient hill of the dead.

He dared not go home. He had not married; he had not left hostages for the King to take. His house and lands would be confiscated, of course, and the excellent painting of Jovan himself as a decrepit octogenarian . . .

But there was money to keep him comfortable for the rest of his life if he could reach Rynildissen. He could buy passage on a ship, if he could reach the docks. Had he enough coins? Never mind; he wore rings; that was what rings were for. He would sell the silver buckles on his shoes if need be.

He passed the tavern, walking faster now. He'd painted that sign himself: the turtle whose shell was the world, afloat in a sea of stars. Real stars were

• 232 •

emerging, and the World-Turtle was noisy and bright with candlelight. *Kassily, we've lost our professions tonight, but you at least will keep your life.*

There were no houses beyond the World-Turtle, and Jovan felt free to run. He had a good view of the castle. Something was happening there. Mounted men galloping down the torchlit drive? But horses wouldn't come here, nor would the Seaclaw folk. He was passing graves already, though nothing marked them but bare rounded earth or thicker grass: the graves of those who could not afford better.

Jovan was panting now. He passed white stones set upright, with marks chiseled into them. Higher up the stones had been hacked into rectangular shape. He could see small buildings, crypts, a miniature city of the dead lined along the crest of Worm's-Head Hill. Already he was wading through thickening mist. The night fog might help him.

Hide in a crypt? He would need shelter. A man could go hungry for a few days. It might do him good; he had fed too well, perhaps, these eight years. Water would be a problem, but this was wet country. There would be dew to collect in the morning.

The crypt he was passing was shoulder-high, built of stone with a stone door barred on the outside. The next was like it. Children's tales spoke of a time when ghosts were deadly dangerous . . . but an outside bar meant that he could get in.

A miniature castle loomed to his right: the royal crypt, centuries old, with (reputedly) plenty of room left for future generations. No guard would enter there. Jovan circled, making for the great stone door that faced the harbor. The fog was thick, waist-high; it rippled as he moved.

Clothes would be a problem when he reached the harbor. He could hardly walk the docks dressed for a ball! But his cloak would hide him long enough . . . and Jovan had begun to think past the next hour of life. That was all to the good.

He slowed to a walk, and a grin began to form as he pictured King Daryanree dancing with fury. None would dare go near; how would they get their orders? Would the Guard even know what they were hunting?

Just before the door, the fog rose up and faced him.

Elsewhere the mist was rising to take other shapes, but Jovan didn't turn his head. This before him was enough: a burly man with a ravaged, eyeless face, six inches broader of shoulder than Jovan and a head taller, wearing the crown of Seaclaw. He leaned on the haft of a two-handed war-axe. The skin of the right arm flapped loose; it had been flayed away nearly to the shoulder. The left hand looked soft, with every bone broken. Loops of . . . what might have been sausage hung below his torso-armor.

The ghost spoke in a voice that seemed to come from miles away. "I know you. Samal! Usurper! I would kill you slowly, but to what point? Time enough to torment you in the ages after you're *dead*," it shrieked, and the war-axe moved with supernatural speed.

Somehow, Jovan hadn't thought of moving.

The axe swung down, split him from crown to crotch and drove deep into the dirt. Jovan felt no sensation at all. The old King stared, aghast. He swung from the side, a blow that would have severed Jovan at the waist. Then he howled and hurled the axe away.

The axe was a wisp of mist. The King, turning toward the crypt, lost shape and became a whorl in the waist-high fog. And a voice behind Jovan said, "He's mad, of course."

"Is he." Jovan turned.

Ghosts formed an arc around him. They watched him solemnly, like the audience that often formed to watch him paint. Some were only an unevenness in the mist layer, mere suggestions of human shape. Others showed detail: men and women ravaged by disease or age; the heads of children just showing above the mist; a burly man who hung back from the crowd, whose rope-burned neck hung askew and whose fingertips dripped big droplets of fog.

The nearest had the shape of a lean old man with pointed nose and chin, bald scalp, a fringe of long hair blurred at the ends: a very clear, precise image. That apparition said, "Zale the Tenth was tortured to death. He lasted ten days. It would have driven anyone mad."

Jovan got his own throat working, largely to see if he could do it. Could he get the ghosts talking? "I take it you got off easier."

"I think not. The plague is an easier death, but it took my family. Will you be here long?"

"A few days."

"Good. We'd like the company, and we won't harm you. Can't."

"The *manna* level's worn too low." Jovan sighed, perhaps in relief; he wasn't sure himself. "Over most of the world ghosts have no power at all. You're the first I've ever seen."

A child's voice asked, "Are you a magician? You talk like one."

"I am," Jovan said.

The old man's ghost drifted toward him. Jovan held himself from flinching at its immaterial touch. The ghost reached into Jovan's chest. Jovan thought he felt cold fingers wrapped around his heart. The ghost grinned (the teeth were missing all down the right side, and scarce on the left) and said, "You're not."

"Why not?"

"A magician keeps some of the magic that passes through him. A touch of *manna* makes a ghost stronger. You don't have any. We all know about *manna* here, but how did you find out?"

Jovan sat down on a headstone. "The old woman who taught me to paint, *she* was a magician. She'd given it up long before I met her, when all the spells gradually stopped working. But Laneerda made her magic by painting. You know, paint a successful hunt, put hairs of the animal and the hunter in the paint. Or paint your own army winning a battle—"

A distant scream caused Jovan to jump. The scream of a horse? Two horses in chorus, down at the foot of the hill.

The specter didn't appear to have noticed. "Hunters still did that when I was a young man," it said. "So you're a painter. Why did you say you were a magician?"

Jovan wore a guilty grin. "Well, the King thinks so."

"So?"

"Maybe he doesn't by now. But he did, for eight years. I came to Seaclaw just four days ahead of the King's thirtieth birthday. I got into the celebration at the palace by painting my landlady's daughter and bringing it as a present.

"King Daryanree wanted a few words with me. He wanted to meet the girl. She wasn't as pretty as I painted her. But I mentioned my teacher Laneerda, and Daryanree knew the name. Legend has her a lot more powerful than she ever was! We talked some more, and I saw how much Daryanree hated the idea of getting old. So I told him I could keep it from happening."

"That sounds dangerous," the ghost pointed out. "Not to mention dishonest."

"But they did it that way! Paint a portrait, put hair and fingernail clippings and blood and urine from the subject in the paint. Do it right, the painting grows old instead of the subject. Of course you

have to guard the painting, because if that gets hurt
. . . but the better the painting is, the better the spell
works. It's not my fault if the magic isn't good anymore. *I'm* good."

"Why didn't you just take the money and run?"

It was strange to be talking to a ring of ghosts
as if they were any normal audience. Strange, and
oddly pleasant, to finally speak his secret where it
could not harm him. "Daryanree isn't a complete
fool. He offered me a house and an annual fee. I
couldn't see any way to turn that down without
making him suspicious, and it was good money. So
I told him it was just as well, because the painting
would have to be tended—even Daryanree knows
that *manna* fades with time—and when I told him
about the old spell I added some details.

"I painted him naked, and I made him shave so
more of his face would show in the painting, otherwise he'd get old under the whiskers. He wouldn't
shave his head. He did agree to keep his face shaved
for the rest of his life. It started a court fashion. I
made him up a fluid to rinse his hair every few days,
to maintain an affinity with the paint—"

"He'll still get old," the ghost protested. "Only
the dead don't get old."

"Well, but I had him washing his hair in berry
juice that turns dark, and there's no gray in his
beard because he shaves it off, and maybe he's getting wrinkled, but who's going to tell him? Nobody
says that to the King! As for the painting, I insisted
on absolute privacy while I renewed the spells. Trust
me, the King's painting did grow older!

"I did some good, too. Daryanree was due to execute a bunch of farmers for not paying their taxes. The hands in the painting showed bloody. I told the King, made him come see. He freed the farmers. When he was ready to declare war on Rynildissen, the painting sprouted a dripping red line across the neck, and his crown and robes turned transparent. That took days. I had to paint it in my house and smuggle it in. But the King signed a peace treaty, and he made me a councillor.

"Then this afternoon the King made an advance to the wrong girl. Right about now he's staring into a mirror and wondering how he could have been so gullible."

"And you came here."

"I thought I'd be safe. I didn't really believe in ghosts. I was sure they couldn't hurt me."

"And now?"

The murmuring around Jovan didn't sound entirely friendly. Nonetheless Jovan said, "It's still the way to bet."

"Do you believe in a finding-stone?"

"Mmm? For finding a man?" Jovan had never heard of such a thing. "Well, it would be magic, of course. It wouldn't work except in a few places . . . Why?"

The elderly ghost said, "I was second in command of Zale the Tenth's forces when I was alive. A lot of us joined the usurper, and that way a lot of blood wasn't spilled, but the plague that followed . . . maybe we brought that on us too. Killing a king carries a curse, and Samal's veins carried no more than a jigger of royal blood. But the Guard had a finding-stone spelled by the wizard Clubfoot himself. The kings of Seaclaw still have it, even if it's lost some of its power."

Jovan felt a numbing fear flowing through his body. "Will they dare come here?"

A voice cleared its throat and said, "I did." It was clearly human and very close.

Jovan didn't turn. A clean swing of a sword through his neck? When the luck turns sour—"Companion of dogs," Jovan whispered to the old man's ghost. "You kept me here. You made me talk. You're dead! You're not an officer anymore, you didn't have to— I didn't do any real harm—" He couldn't speak further, his tongue was too thick.

Something massive moved through the ring of ghosts, and their bodies swirled and steadied as it passed. Jovan stood up to face a man of the King's Guard.

Daryanree chose his guards partly for their appearance. The man was tall; he fitted his armor well. He carried a well-polished, well-honed sword in one hand and what might have been a large volcanic-glass arrowhead in the open palm of the other.

But he was alone. No horse would walk among ghosts and no companion had followed, and he must be half out of his mind with fear. Jovan could smell chilled fear-sweat. And Jovan cried piteously, "I can't move! They've got me, but it's not too late for you. Run!"

There was a tremor in the burly guard's voice.

"These specters are my own people, barbarian! I heard what you said. The King wants to talk to you. Will you come quietly?"

A king cannot afford to look the fool. Jovan knew too much to live.

He said, "Yes! Yes, if you can pull me loose from this." He let his eyes roll; he stretched his arms toward the guard; he writhed on the headstone, then sagged in defeat.

"Liar!" the guard roared. He moved forward as if through glue. Jovan waited to see if the guard would break.

The mist surged up, and Zale the Tenth stood before the guard. The skin of his arm flapped as he moved. Massive, flayed and blind and tormented, the old king's ghost was a horrid sight. "I know you," it cried. "Samal! Usurper!" The war-axe rose and fell.

The guard tried to riposte. The axe wafted through his sword and smashed his naked shield-arm back across his chest. The guard reeled backward and smacked against the rough stone of a crypt.

Jovan shook his head.

The guard didn't move. And the fog had clumped above him, nearly hiding him. Ghosts surrounded the man like jackals feeding. Jovan remembered other legends, of vampires—

He forced himself to move among them, through them, feeling resistance and chill. He unlaced the guard's leather torso armor and pulled it off and placed his palm on the man's chest.

"His heart's still beating. I don't understand," the artist said, and sudden claustrophobic terror took him. He could see nothing; he was embedded in ghosts.

The finding-stone was shattered in the guard's hand. The magic in it could have made Zale's axe real enough to hurt, real enough to send a man flying backward. But there was no blood, no break in the armor or the tunic beneath or, when Jovan carefuly pulled the tunic off, in the skin either. Not real enough to cut, then. A bruise was forming above the sternum, but Jovan found no broken ribs.

"Bumped his head," Jovan mumbled. He found blood on the back of the man's scalp, but no splintered softness beneath. "He'll wake soon. I've got to get moving. They think the stone will find me. They won't look for me at the docks—"

"They'll look," said the old Guard officer's voice.

Jovan stripped hurriedly. The touch of the ghosts was cold, and they clustered close. He donned the guard's clothing as rapidly as he could. The boots were roomy; he tore up his own shirt to pad them. His rings he took off and put in the toes. His cloak wouldn't fit the look of the uniform. He spread it over the guard.

He strode out of the mist of ghosts. The fog ran away from him downhill, to form a pale carpet over the harbor and the sea. The lighthouse on Seaclaw Point showed above. Jovan took it as his target.

The dead general took shape, striding alongside him, clutching something. It said briskly, "They'll look. I'll follow you and point you out."

Jovan stopped. He said, "You can't leave Worm's-Head Hill. You never could before and you can't now."

"Do you believe that?"

With the magic of the finding-stone to give them life, ghosts could harm him now. When the luck turns sour . . . but luck had saved him from the guard. Push it, then!

He snatched at the ghost's clenched fist. The bones of his hand passed with a grating sensation through other bones, and tore away two shards of black glass, two pieces of the broken finding-stone. Jovan flung them far into the dark. The ghost ran after them. Jovan ran the other way, downhill toward the light.

ABOUT THE AUTHORS

Author of such classics as *Ringworld* and *Ringworld Engineers*; co-author of bestsellers like *The Mote in God's Eye*, *Lucifer's Hammer*, and *Footfall*; Nebula winner and five-time recipient of SF's Hugo Award, LARRY NIVEN is known to millions as "the premier writer of hard science fiction." Niven lives in California.

STEVEN BARNES is a man of many parts. He has written for television and the big screen, and is the author of *Streetlethal*, *Gorgon Child*, and *The Kundalini Equation* (all published by Tor Books), as well as the co-author (with Larry Niven) of such best-selling collaborations as *Dream Park*, *The Barsoom Project* and *The Descent of Anansi*, and *The Legacy of Heorot*, written with Niven and Jerry Pournelle. His short stories and non-fiction pieces have been widely published. He has taught creative writing, hosted talk shows and holds advanced degrees in the martial arts.

Steven Barnes on
Larry Niven

About 11 years ago I'd done a lot of writing but the only payment I'd received was something like ⅕ of a cent a word or payment in contributor's copies. Still I considered myself a writer.

So one day I'm in the clubhouse of the Los Angeles Science Fiction Society, and Larry Niven walks in. When Larry walks in, you understand, he is completely surrounded by the people there. It's like he's a god, and this is his domain.

I walked up to him and said: "Hello, Mr. Niven, my name's Steven Barnes, and I'm a writer."

He took a puff on his pipe, looked at me and said: "Okay, tell me a story."

I just about died. But it so happened I'd sent out a story earlier that day about a compulsive gambler who pawns his pacemaker, and somehow I stumbled through it.

After that we started talking. He seemed kind

of reserved, but even then I could see he was still in touch with his child-personality. I could especially see it in his eyes. In some ways it was as if the beard and pipe were props to convince you that, yes, these are the badges of adulthood. But back there were these little boy's eyes.

I asked him if he'd read a story, and he said he would, and the next week I gave him an envelope containing three. I saw him the week following and asked if he had read them, and he said, yes, Jerry Pournelle and he had both read them. He said he was intrigued and asked me whether I'd be interested in looking at a story he'd tried writing ten years before and hadn't been able to complete to his satisfaction.

Thank God the problems with the story had nothing to do with astrophysics or any of the technical things that Larry is a master of. They had to do with the way the human beings were relating to one another, and I was able to fix it.

We've been collaborating ever since.

The imperative for men in our culture is that they must go out and create—work, produce, change the land around them. Now people often think that it's easy when you have a lot of money handed to you as a kid, as Larry had. All that does is say to you that the chances are very good you'll never live up to the man who created all that wealth.

But Larry created a career separate from anything his family had handed him. He could have taken their money and lain by the side of the pool and vegetated or put it into land or condominiums and made a lot of money. And, indeed, he has made money off the money his father handed him. But the most important thing Larry did was to go out and define a whole new world. If his world in California had already been conquered, then Larry would create new worlds to conquer and people them with his own creations.

—from a conversation with Steven Barnes

THE BEST IN
SCIENCE FICTION

☐	54310-6	A FOR ANYTHING	$3.95
☐	54311-4	*Damon Knight*	Canada $4.95
☐	55625-9	BRIGHTNESS FALLS FROM THE AIR	$3.50
☐	55626-7	*James Tiptree, Jr.*	Canada $3.95
☐	53815-3	CASTING FORTUNE	$3.95
☐	53816-1	*John M. Ford*	Canada $4.95
☐	50554-9	THE ENCHANTMENTS OF FLESH & SPIRIT	$3.95
☐	50555-7	*Storm Constantine*	Canada $4.95
☐	55413-2	HERITAGE OF FLIGHT	$3.95
☐	55414-0	*Susan Shwartz*	Canada $4.95
☐	54293-2	LOOK INTO THE SUN	$3.95
☐	54294-0	*James Patrick Kelly*	Canada $4.95
☐	54925-2	MIDAS WORLD	$2.95
☐	54926-0	*Frederik Pohl*	Canada $3.50
☐	53157-4	THE SECRET ASCENSION	$4.50
☐	53158-2	*Michael Bishop*	Canada $5.50
☐	55627-5	THE STARRY RIFT	$4.50
☐	55628-3	*James Tiptree, Jr.*	Canada $5.50
☐	50623-5	TERRAPLANE	$3.95
☐		*Jack Womack*	Canada $4.95
☐	50369-4	WHEEL OF THE WINDS	$3.95
☐	50370-8	*M.J. Engh*	Canada $4.95

Buy them at your local bookstore or use this handy coupon:
Clip and mail this page with your order.

Publishers Book and Audio Mailing Service
P.O. Box 120159, Staten Island, NY 10312-0004

Please send me the book(s) I have checked above. I am enclosing $ _____
(Please add $1.25 for the first book, and $.25 for each additional book to cover postage and handling.
Send check or money order only—no CODs.)

Name _____

Address _____

City _____ State/Zip _____

Please allow six weeks for delivery. Prices subject to change without notice.

TOR SCIENCE FICTION DOUBLES

☐	50010-5	THE BLIND GEOMETER	Robinson	$3.50
☐	50114-4	THE NEW ATLANTIS	LeGuin	Canada $4.50
☐	55952-5	BORN WITH THE DEAD	Silverberg	$2.95
☐	55953-3	THE SALIVA TREE	Aldiss	Canada $3.95
☐	55964-9	THE COLOR OF NEANDERTHAL EYES	Tiptree	$3.50
☐	50204-3	AND STRANGE AT ECBATAN THE TREES	Bishop	Canada $4.50
☐	50362-7	DIVIDE AND RULE	de Camp	$3.50
☐	50363-5	THE SWORD OF RHIANNON	Brackett	Canada $4.50
☐	50275-2	ELEGY FOR ANGELS AND DOGS	Williams	$3.50
☐		THE GRAVEYARD HEART	Zelazny	Canada $4.50
☐	55963-0	ENEMY MINE	Longyear	$2.95
☐	54302-5	ANOTHER ORPHAN	Kessel	Canada $3.95
☐	50854-8	EYE FOR EYE	Card	$3.95
☐		THE TUNESMITH	Biggle	Canada $4.95
☐	50813-0	FUGUE STATE	Ford	$3.50
☐		THE DEATH OF DOCTOR ISLAND	Wolfe	Canada $4.50
☐	55971-1	HARDFOUGHT	Bear	$3.50
☐	55951-7	CASCADE POINT	Zahn	Canada $4.50
☐	55879-0	HE WHO SHAPES	Zelazny	$2.95
☐	50266-3	THE INFINITY BOX	Wilhelm	Canada $3.95
☐	50983-8	HOME IS THE HANGMAN	Zelazny	$3.50
☐		WE, IN SOME STRANGE POWER'S EMPLOY,		Canada $4.50
		MOVE ON A RIGOROUS LINE	Delany	

Buy them at your local bookstore or use this handy coupon:
Clip and mail this page with your order.

Publishers Book and Audio Mailing Service
P.O. Box 120159, Staten Island, NY 10312-0004

Please send me the book(s) I have checked above. I am enclosing $ _____
(Please add $1.25 for the first book, and $.25 for each additional book to cover postage and handling.
Send check or money order only—no CODs.)

Name _____
Address _____
City _____ State/Zip _____

Please allow six weeks for delivery. Prices subject to change without notice.

BESTSELLERS
FROM TOR

☐ ☐	50570-0	ALL ABOUT WOMEN *Andrew M. Greeley*	$4.95 Canada $5.95
☐ ☐	58341-8 58342-6	ANGEL FIRE *Andrew M. Greeley*	$4.95 Canada $5.95
☐ ☐	52725-9 52726-7	BLACK WIND *F. Paul Wilson*	$4.95 Canada $5.95
☐ ☐	51392-4	LONG RIDE HOME *W. Michael Gear*	$4.95 Canada $5.95
☐ ☐	50350-3	OKTOBER *Stephen Gallagher*	$4.95 Canada $5.95
☐ ☐	50857-2	THE RANSOM OF BLACK STEALTH One *Dean Ing*	$5.95 Canada $6.95
☐ ☐	50088-1	SAND IN THE WIND *Kathleen O'Neal Gear*	$4.50 Canada $5.50
☐ ☐	51878-0	SANDMAN *Linda Crockett*	$4.95 Canada $5.95
☐ ☐	50214-0 50215-9	THE SCHOLARS OF NIGHT *John M. Ford*	$4.95 Canada $5.95
☐ ☐	51826-8	TENDER PREY *Julia Grice*	$4.95 Canada $5.95
☐ ☐	52188-4	TIME AND CHANCE *Alan Brennert*	$4.95 Canada $5.95

Buy them at your local bookstore or use this handy coupon:
Clip and mail this page with your order.

Publishers Book and Audio Mailing Service
P.O. Box 120159, Staten Island, NY 10312-0004

Please send me the book(s) I have checked above. I am enclosing $ _____
(please add $1.25 for the first book, and $.25 for each additional book to cover postage and handling.
Send check or money order only—no CODs).

Name _____
Address _____
City _____ State/Zip _____
Please allow six weeks for delivery. Prices subject to change without notice.